PART ONE

W9-CFU-944

BALLET

Annabel Thomas
Edited by Helen Davies
Designed by Chris Scollen

Contents

Ballet consultant: Kate Castle

Illustrated by Ann Savage, Peter Mennim, Chris Lyon, Kathy Wyatt and Cathy Wood.

What is ballet?

Ballet is a way of telling a story using music and dance instead of words. It consists of patterns of movement which have developed over the centuries. The word classical describes its style. This part of the book is all about classical ballet. Some of the influences which have helped to make up classical ballet are shown on the right.

Dancers who perform ballet on stage are highly trained. Many people learn the techniques of ballet for fun, though. It helps them to feel graceful, co-ordinated and fit.

Classical ballet is found all around the world, for instance in Europe, the USA, China, Japan and South America.

19th century ballroom dancing.

Classical ballet.

Elizabethan dancing.

Classical ballet

Early classical ballets such as *Giselle* and *La Sylphide* were created during the Romantic Movement in the first half of the 19th century. This movement influenced art, music and ballet. It was concerned with the supernatural world of spirits and magic. It often showed women as passive and fragile. These themes are reflected in the ballets of the time, called Romantic ballets.

Ballets created during the latter half of the 19th century, such as *Swan Lake, The Nutcracker* and *The Sleeping Beauty* represent classical ballet in the grandest form.* Their main aim was to display the techniques of classical ballet to the full.

In these ballets, complicated sequences which show off demanding steps, leaps and turns are fitted into the story.

Ballets created during this century are called Modern ballets. They do not always have a definite story line. They have a theme, though, and concentrate more on emotions and atmospheres and attempt to arouse feelings in the audience. Different people might react to them in different ways.

Romantic, Classical and Modern ballets all follow the techniques of classical ballet.

2 *This book calls ballets of this period Classical ballets, with a capital C.

Court dancing of the 15th and 16th centuries.

Folk dancing.

How ballet began

Beauchamps

The roots of classical ballet go back 500 years. It began in the courts of Italian noblemen and soon spread to the French courts. Performers danced, sang and recited poetry to entertain guests at celebrations.

The first real ballet, where mime, music and dance were combined in one performance, was called *The Comic Ballet of the Queen*. It was staged in 1581 at the French court.

Court dancer.

Louis XIV of France founded the first ballet school, called the Royal Academy of Dancing, in 1661. A ballet master at the Academy, called Beauchamps, established five positions of the feet. These are still the basis of all ballet steps.*

Other steps came from Elizabethan and folk dances. The more acrobatic steps developed from the antics of street players and circus performers and from the Italian theatre, called *La Commedia del Arte*.

When ballets were first performed, men played the female parts, disguising themselves in wigs and masks. Women were allowed to dance in public after 1681. However, they had to wear lots of bulky clothes which hampered movement.

The possibility for spectacular footwork emerged when Marie Camargo daringly shortened her dress above her ankles in the 1720s.

Shorter dress revealing ankles.

About this book

This book is both about doing ballet yourself and enjoying ballet as a member of the audience. Here are some of the things that you can find out about in the book.

You can find out what happens at a ballet class and there are step-by-step instructions for how to do some basic ballet steps.

At the end of the book, lots of ballet words are explained.

The book explains what goes on behind the scenes when a major ballet is staged. You can also find out all about wigs, costumes and how stage make-up is applied to create different characters.

The work of a choreographer, who combines dance, music and mime to create a ballet, is described. You can find out about recording ballets by writing them down, called dance notation.

There are suggestions for what to look out for when you watch a ballet and tips on where to sit in a theatre. You can find the stories of some of the most famous ballets towards the end of the book.

*You can find out what these five positions are on page 6.

Getting started

You can start ballet classes at any age, though the younger you are, the more easily your body adapts to the physical demands that ballet makes. Children of three years old can go to simple dance classes. Proper ballet lessons begin at the age of seven.

Classes are held at dancing schools, community centres and some sports centres. It is important to find a qualified teacher who will teach you the correct technique. He or she will have letters after his or her name, such as AISTD.*

What to wear

In a ballet class, you wear layers of clothing. These keep you warm when you start and you can strip them off as you get hotter. The clothes are close-fitting so the lines and shapes your body makes can easily be seen by the teacher.

Girls usually wear a leotard and pink tights which allow for plenty of freedom of movement. At the beginning of a class you may like to wear legwarmers and a crossover. This is a type of cardigan that crosses over at the front and ties at the back.

Boys wear black tights with white socks over the top and a white T shirt. You can wear a track suit until you have warmed up.

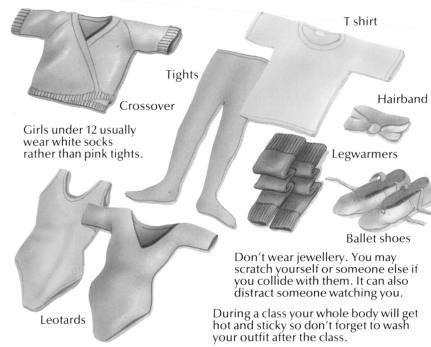

T shirt

Tights

Crossover

Girls under 12 usually wear white socks rather than pink tights.

Hairband

Legwarmers

Ballet shoes

Leotards

Don't wear jewellery. You may scratch yourself or someone else if you collide with them. It can also distract someone watching you.

During a class your whole body will get hot and sticky so don't forget to wash your outfit after the class.

How to wear your hair

Your hair needs to be off your face so it does not get in the way or make your neck hot. Most girls with long hair put it up in a bun held in a hair net, with a hairband to stop wisps flying out. You could also plait it round your head. If you have short hair you can wear a hairband to stop it falling forwards. Boys can wear sweatbands in class for the same reason.

These styles allow your whole face to be seen and give you a long neck line.

Buying your outfit

You do not need to buy any special clothing until you have been to a ballet class and know that you like it and want to carry on. Most teachers will not mind if you start in bare feet, wearing a track suit or swimming costume.

Ask your teacher where is the best place to buy your equipment. Most big department stores sell leotards, tights and track suits. You can get ballet shoes from most shoe shops.

*Associate of the Imperial Society of Teachers of Dancing.

4

Ballet shoes

Boys wear shoes made of soft leather, held on by elastic. Girls' shoes are made of leather or satin, kept on by elastic or ribbons tied round the ankle. You can find out how to sew on ribbons and elastic below.

A girl does not need block toed ballet shoes, called *pointe* shoes, until her teacher considers her feet and legs strong enough to dance on her toes (*en pointe*).

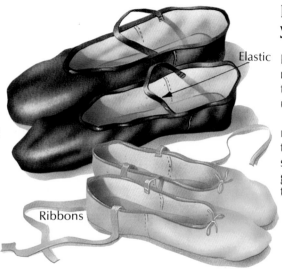

Elastic

Ribbons

Looking after your shoes

Ballet shoes are hand-made and expensive, so take care of them. Only use them for classes.

You can clean the ribbons by scrubbing them with a nail brush, soap and water. Do not get the shoes themselves wet.

Sewing on ribbons

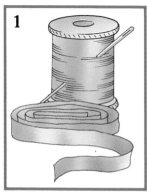
1

For each shoe, you need a strong ribbon with a non-slippery back, about 1cm (½in) wide and 1m (1yd) long.

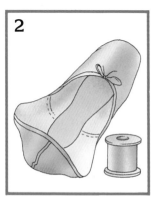
2

To find out where the ribbon should be sewn, fold the heel forward along the sole, as shown.

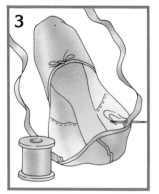
3

Position the ends of the ribbon on the inside of the shoe, either side of the fold. Then sew them firmly into place.

4

If you are using elastic, sew it in the same place as the ribbon.

Finally, stretch out the loop of ribbon and cut it in the middle to make two ribbons of the same length.

Tying the ribbon

When you tie the ribbons of your shoes, your foot should be flat on the floor.

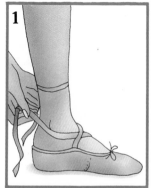
1

Bring both ribbons forward, cross them over and take them behind your ankle.

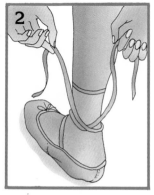
2

Cross the ribbons over behind your ankle. Then bring them round to the front again.

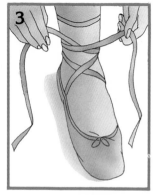
3

Cross the ribbons over once again at the front, a little above the first crossing.

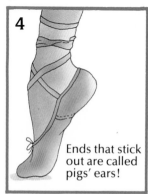
4

Ends that stick out are called pigs' ears!

Finally, knot the ribbons twice at the back and neatly tuck in the loose ends.

Ballet techniques

These two pages tell you some facts about ballet which you need to know before learning any steps. You can find out about the five positions of the feet and the seven movements of dance, which are the basis of all ballet steps.

All ballet steps have French names. This is because many steps were first introduced at the Academy of Dancing founded by King Louis XIV of France. In this book, the French names of the steps are in italics.

The five positions of the feet

Nearly every step in ballet begins and ends with one of five positions of the feet. They were devised by King Louis XIV's ballet master, Beauchamps. He worked them out so that a person's weight would be evenly placed no matter what position their body was in.

To start with, you will only use the first, second and third positions. Later, you will learn fourth and fifth and use third less. There are two fourth positions, one open and one crossed. To begin with you will probably mostly use open fourth.

First position
(en première)

Place your heels together and turn your feet and legs out to the sides.

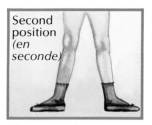

Second position (en seconde)

Place your feet apart by about one and a half times your foot's length. Turn them out.

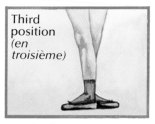

Third position (en troisième)

Put the heel of one foot against the middle of the other foot. Turn both feet out.

Open fourth (en quatrième: ouverte)

Place one foot directly forward from first position by about ⅓m (1ft).

Crossed fourth (en quatrième: croisée)

In crossed fourth, one foot goes directly forward from fifth (see next picture).

Fifth position (en cinquième)

Turn both feet out, with the heel of one foot against the toes of your other foot.

Turn-out

In ballet, the feet and legs have to be turned out from the hips so that your toes and knees face sideways instead of forwards. This is called turn-out. It takes years of practice to do it properly.

Dancers first began to turn out their legs in Louis XIV's day. It showed off the calves and elegant, heeled shoes of the male dancers. Turn-out is now essential to the technique of classical ballet.

Turning your legs out enables you to lift them higher. Without it your hip joints would lock up at a certain height and the streamlined look of ballet would be impossible to achieve.

The seven movements of dance

Every step in ballet is based on one of seven dance movements. These are movements which your body can make naturally. Their French names are shown below with their English translation opposite.

Plier — to bend
Glisser — to glide
Tourner — to turn
Etendre — to stretch
Sauter — to jump
Relever — to rise
Elancer — to dart

These words are not always used in the form shown. For instance, *tendu* or *tendue* means stretched.

You can check the meaning of French words in the list of ballet words on pages 47-48.

Darting

Gliding

Bending

Stretching

Turning

Rising

Jumping

Using the seven movements

Here are some examples of ballet steps and the different movements that they use. You can find out how to do some of these steps yourself on pages 30-35.

Arabesque penché

This is called an *arabesque penché*. It combines stretching and raising.

Pas de chat

This step is called a *pas de chat* (step of a cat). You dart and jump like a pouncing cat.

Glissade

A *glissade* is a step where your foot glides along the ground with your knees bent.

Pirouette

A *pirouette* is a turning step. You turn on one leg, bend the other leg and lift it.

Classical ballet techniques

Within classical ballet there are different techniques, such as the Royal Academy of Dancing (R.A.D.), the British Ballet Organisation (B.B.O.) and the Cecchetti Society techniques. You can be examined in these techniques. There is also the Imperial Society Classical Ballet exam syllabus.

The basic movements are the same in all techniques but the combinations of steps vary and some of the arm positions differ slightly.

Going to a class

When you begin to learn ballet you should attend one or two classes a week. Regular attendance will gradually improve your technique. Professional dancers have to go to at least a class a day, as well as rehearsals, to keep in top condition and constantly to improve their ballet skills.

The picture below shows the inside of a ballet studio. At the bottom of the page you can find what to expect when you go to a class. Opposite you can see the different kinds of steps you will learn.

A wooden hand rail, called a *barre*, runs round the wall at waist level. You hold on to it for certain exercises (see next page).

Some studios have two *barres*, one higher than the other, for people of different heights.

There are full length mirrors on the wall so you can watch yourself when you dance and correct any mistakes.

This is a box of rosin. Rosin is a yellow crystal made from the sap of fir trees. If you rub the soles of your shoes in it, it breaks up into a white powder which sticks to them and stops you slipping.

There is usually a dressing room where you can leave your outdoor clothes and get changed before and after class.

A pianist usually accompanies the classes. This helps the students perform the exercises at the right pace and develops their sense of rhythm.

If there is no piano your teacher will probably use a tape recorder. Most teachers prefer a pianist, though, as he or she can adjust the speed of the music to the exercises and stop and start without delays.

A proper ballet studio has a floor with a wooden or vinyl surface. The floor is sprung which means that it "gives" very slightly beneath your feet when you jump.

What happens at a class?

All classes, no matter how advanced, follow roughly the same structure. They start with exercises at the *barre*, followed by "centre practice" (see next page) and end with jumps, turns and travelling steps.

At first you will be put in a beginners' class. Your teacher will stand where everyone can see him or her. The teacher will show how each step is done and then go around the class correcting students' movements.

Warming up at the *barre*

A class begins with gentle exercises to "warm up" your muscles, stretching them and preparing them for more demanding movements. This reduces the risk of you hurting yourself.

You warm up at the *barre*, beginning with *pliés* (knee bends). You can find out how to do *pliés* on pages 26-27.

Further exercises use your feet, ankles, knees and whole leg in more strenuous movements.

The *barre* acts as a support so you can concentrate on the alignment of one part of your body with another in harmony and balance. This is called placing.

To help your placing, imagine a line running straight down through the centre of your body, ending between your feet. Then imagine another line going straight across your hips, so both hips are level with each other.

Centre practice

You move into the middle of the room for centre practice. Here you learn how to hold your arms, called *port de bras*.

You also repeat some of the foot and leg exercises done at the *barre*, to develop strength and muscles without its support.

You then progress to more sustained movements, where, for example, you slowly raise your leg. (See pages 30-31.)

Jumps, turns and travelling steps

The latter part of the class consists of *petit allegro* and then *grand allegro*. *Allegro** is Italian for quick. *Petit* and *grand* are French for small and big.

Petit allegro consists of small jumping and turning steps. *Grand allegro* is large jumping and travelling steps. There is more about these on pages 32-35.

How to stand

Learning to stand correctly can take a lot of practice. Your head should be held up with your chin level. Relax your shoulders to lengthen your neck.

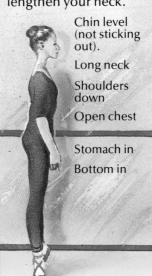

Chin level (not sticking out).

Long neck

Shoulders down

Open chest

Stomach in

Bottom in

Your stomach and bottom should be well tucked in. Carry your weight on the balls of your feet so that your heels touch the floor but do not dig in.

*Allegro is a musical term. These are always written in Italian.

Creating a ballet

The art of creating a ballet is called choreography. Someone who does this is called a choreographer. As well as new ballets, a choreographer may develop a new version of an old ballet.

Most ballet companies employ a choreographer. New ballets keep the dancers in the company enthusiastic and keep audiences interested in the company.

A ballet may tell a story or create a particular atmosphere. Nowadays, though, some ballets are devoted to movement for its own sake.

The idea for a new ballet may be sparked off by a poem, piece of music, story, play, painting, or even a single dancer's talent.

The dancer Lynn Seymour inspired the choreographer

Kenneth MacMillan to create works for her. The American contemporary dance choreographer, Twyla Tharp, created works for the classical dancer, Mikhail Barishnikov.

How choreographers work

Choreographers are usually trained dancers with first-hand knowledge of the steps they use. They begin by getting to know the music for a new ballet before starting work with the dancers.

Most choreographers first work out what effects they want to achieve, with a framework of steps. Then they work on the steps with the dancers to find the best movements.

Choreographers seldom work straight through a ballet. They usually begin with parts for one or two dancers. Then they develop the small group dances and leave the big groups until last.

Most companies have resident ballet teachers. They watch the choreographer at work so that they get to know the steps of a new ballet. This means they can rehearse the dancers later.

As a ballet is choreographed, the steps are recorded in a kind of shorthand called notation so that they are not forgotten. You can find out more about ballet notation on pages 12-13.

Costume and scenery must be in keeping with the style of a ballet and the choreographer's intentions. The choreographer and designer work together in planning how a ballet should look.

Music for ballets

A choreographer may like to work with a composer, so that music is composed with a ballet in mind. The choreographer Wayne Eagling worked with the "pop" composer Vangelis on the synthesized music for Eagling's ballet, *Frankenstein*.

Alternatively, a choreographer will find a piece of music that inspires him or her. George Balanchine created his ballet *Violin Concerto* in response to the composer Stravinsky's violin concerto.

Sometimes existing pieces of music are arranged specially for new ballets. Composer Branwell Tovey arranged several pieces of Mussorgsky's music for David Bintley's ballet *Snow Queen*, so that all the steps fitted exactly.

Using steps in different ways

A ballet is similar to a piece of music. Sequences of steps are repeated and varied, just as tunes reoccur in a movement of music. Steps may be danced alone and then with a partner, just as different parts of the orchestra pick up and repeat a tune. The same step used differently can portray a variety of emotions.

First *arabesque en pointe*.

First *arabesque on demi-plié*.

Second *arabesque*.

A first *arabesque en pointe* can give the impression of strength and vitality, as danced by the Black Swan in the ballet *Swan Lake*. The same step looks much gentler on a *plié* with the foot flat. The step is used like this in the ballet *Giselle*.

Yet another mood is created by swapping the position of the arms and straightening the knee. A line is now formed along one side of the body creating a feeling of elegance or longing.

A *grand jeté* is a very dramatic leap through the air with legs outstretched. It can suggest different qualities, such as strength and exuberance. In *Coppélia*, Swanhilda leaps with her arms raised above her head, conveying joy and happiness.

Writing steps down

The art of recording a ballet or dance in a written code is called choreology. It is also sometimes called notation.

Before the skill was developed at the beginning of this century, ballets were only kept alive by constantly being danced. Some people attempted to keep written records of steps but these were often only understood by the writer. As a result, many ballets of the 19th century and earlier have been lost.

Nowadays most companies record, catalogue and store their ballets. This means a ballet can be staged by other companies throughout the world.

Dance notation

There are two methods of dance notation recognized throughout the ballet world.

One is called Labanotation, named after its inventor Rudolf von Laban.

The other is Benesh notation, named after Rudolf and Joan Benesh, who devised it.

Both methods can indicate any movement and position of the body and record whole ballets accurately.

Benesh notation

Benesh notation was developed in the late 1940s. Rudolf Benesh was an artist and Joan Benesh was a dancer. The idea for the code grew out of their joint desire to record movement on paper.

Nowadays dance students learn Benesh notation as part of their training. You can find out how Benesh notation works on the opposite page.

Labanotation

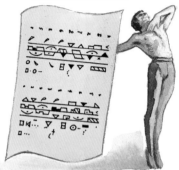

Laban devised Labanotation to record a style of movement which he began to develop in 1910. It is mainly used for contemporary dance.*

What is a choreologist?

A person who records ballets is called a choreologist. Choreologists are trained dancers. They record new ballets as they are rehearsed and old ballets for future reference.

They may take early rehearsals of old ballets that are being restaged. They read the notated records and teach the dancers the steps.

Using video

Nowadays ballet companies usually make video recordings to support the work of the choreologist. While the notation records the steps of a ballet, the video records a particular interpretation of it.

Video is also used as a teaching device, helping dancers to learn a role.

How Benesh notation works

Like music, Benesh signs are written on a stave (five parallel lines).

They can be written on a sheet of music on a stave below the music. This means the movements can be read together with the music and shows how the steps correspond to it.

Positions are recorded by drawing dashes and other signs in an imaginary square on the stave. Each line of

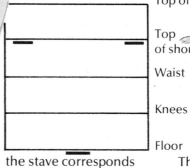

the stave corresponds to a different part of the body. Signs mark the exact spot occupied by the hands and feet.

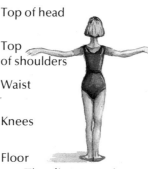

The diagrams view the dancer from behind so signs on the left represent the dancer's left arm and leg.

The basic signs

— Level with body

| In front of body

● Behind body

Different signs show whether the hands and feet are in front or behind the body, or on a line level with it. The signs are shown above.

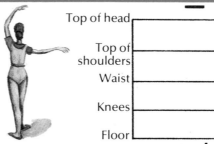

To show feet in fourth, right foot in front and arms as shown, you put an upright dash for the right foot and a dot for the left foot.

Dashes above the head and below the shoulder line represent the hands.

The feet

If feet are flat on the ground, the signs are below the base line. If they are *en pointe*, the signs go above the base line. Feet *en demi-pointe* (half point, or tiptoe) are indicated by signs through the base line. Feet together are shown by one long dash, rather than two separate ones.

Bending

╋ Level with body

╪ In front of body

✕ Behind body

A bent knee is indicated by a cross. There are three different types of cross depending on whether the knee is bent in front, behind or level with the body.

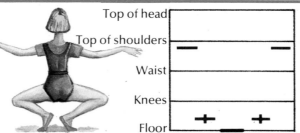

This picture shows a *grand-plié* with feet in first position.

To record it, you put a dash through the base

line (feet together *en demi-pointe*) and crosses for the knees. Dashes show the position of the hands.

The arms

There is no need to record the slight curve of the arms which is natural in ballet. However, a big bend in an elbow is recorded with a cross, just like a knee bend. The type of cross you use depends on where the elbow is placed in relation to the rest of the body.

Continuous movement

Professional choreologists often need to record fast, continuous movement quickly. Instead of indicating a raise of the leg for example, by a series of dashes, which would take some time, they trace the path of the leg with one continuous line.

This diagram shows how a step called a *grand battement à la seconde* is recorded using a single line.

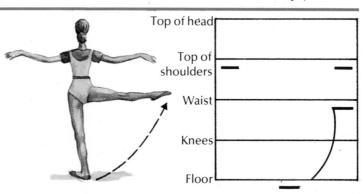

The structure of a ballet company

On these two pages you can see how a ballet company is made up and about the stages in a ballet dancer's career.

Most dancers start their careers by dancing in large groups. Those that show particular talent may be given small parts with solos to dance. Very few are ever good enough to dance the main parts in ballets.

The *corps de ballet*

The *corps de ballet* is a large group of dancers who perform together. In story ballets they dance as fairies, swans, village folk, courtiers and so on. In some Modern ballets they dance in group formations called *ensembles*.

Coryphées

Coryphée comes from the Greek word *koros* and means the leader of a chorus. In ballet, *coryphées* are the leaders of the *corps de ballet*. They may also play character roles or take small parts in story ballets.

Becoming a *coryphée* may be a step to becoming a soloist. However, some experienced dancers, who will never be soloists, are given the title in recognition of their skill.

In *The Sleeping Beauty*, fairy-tale characters like Red Riding Hood and the Wolf are *coryphées*.

Soloists

A soloist dances alone, or solo, in a ballet. He or she usually dances important but not leading roles.

In *The Sleeping Beauty*, the Fairy of Modesty dances a solo when she brings a gift for the christening of Princess Aurora (the Sleeping Beauty). In *Swan Lake* a soloist dances the part of the Black Swan, the evil swan queen.

Very few dancers reach the level of soloist.

Principals

A principal is someone who dances a leading role in a ballet. For example, in *Swan Lake*, Prince Siegfried is the male principal role and Odette, the princess in the guise of a swan, is the female principal role.

Senior principals, who are older members of the company, usually take important character roles. These may be physically less demanding yet require great skill in interpreting the characters. The Ugly Sisters in *Cinderella* are played by senior male principals.

A principal ballerina is sometimes called a *prima ballerina*. The male equivalent is *premier danseur* but the term is rarely used.

The timing and positioning of each member of the *corps de ballet* must be perfect, or the whole effect looks ragged.

A female dancer of soloist or principal status can be given the title of ballerina.

It takes years of hard work to become a principal. Only those with exceptional talent, a brilliant technique and perfect physique ever succeed.

Behind the scenes

This section is about the people who work backstage, alongside the dancers. It tells you about their jobs and describes how everyone works together to make the day to day running of a company go smoothly.

Artistic director

The artistic director plans what ballets will be performed and decides who will dance each role. He or she also employs choreographers to create new ballets. Most ballet companies have at least one full-time choreographer.

Teachers and physiotherapists

Most companies have a ballet master or mistress to rehearse ballets and supervise the *corps de ballet*. A *répétiteur* also rehearses ballets. One or two teachers take daily classes and give individual coaching.

A physiotherapist treats dancers' injuries.

Wardrobe

In the Wardrobe department, a wardrobe master looks after male costumes and a wardrobe mistress takes care of female costumes. Wardrobe assistants wash and repair outfits. There is also a wig master or mistress, who is often a trained hairdresser.

Orchestra

A ballet company has its own orchestra. The conductor and members of the orchestra work under a musical director who is in charge of music for ballets, rehearsals and classes. The conductor rehearses the orchestra and is responsible for their playing.

Stage management

The technical director and stage manager co-ordinate the lighting staff, orchestra, dancers and stage crew. The stage crew are responsible for the electrics, such as wiring and special effects, as well as the props.

Publicity

A press officer stays in contact with the press, informing them of future performances.

A marketing officer commissions posters, leaflets and programmes advertising ballets.*

Some companies have an education or outreach officer, who builds up new audiences by working in schools and the community.

Choreologists and archivists

Most companies have a choreologist to record and teach ballets. They also employ an archivist who collects photos, programmes and press cuttings relating to the company.

Administration

The administrative director is responsible for major policy decisions which can affect the company's public image. Administrative assistants and clerical staff carry out the decisions.

A company also has a general manager who arranges tours, salaries and general business matters.

*You can find out more about publicity on page 17.

Putting on a ballet

Putting a ballet on stage involves an enormous amount of work from many different people. On these two pages you can find out who is involved and what they do.

Dancers rehearsing a ballet.

The dancers

Dancers start rehearsing a new ballet at least six months before its first performance. An existing ballet is prepared for the stage in a matter of weeks.

Schedules for rehearsals are displayed on "call sheets".

Usually four people learn each part. Roles like Princess Aurora in *The Sleeping Beauty* are too demanding for one person to dance every night, so dancers take it in turns. If a principal is ill, young dancers may get the chance to make their début.

The orchestra

To begin with, the orchestra rehearse the music separately from the dancers. When the dancers are familiar with their steps, they rehearse with the orchestra. The musicians have to get used to changes in tempo (speed) which different parts of the ballet demand.

The set and costumes

The set (the scenery on the stage) and costumes* play a major part in creating the atmosphere of a ballet. They are worked out by a designer in conversation with the choreographer.

Scale model of a set.

The background scene may be painted on to a backcloth or it may be made out of wood, with windows and doors through which dancers can enter and leave.

To get an idea of the overall effect of a set before it is built, an accurate scale model may be built.

Lighting

Stage lights are hung above the stage and in the auditorium. They can create impressions such as a sunrise or sunset. In *Petrushka*, blue lights are used to give the impression of a Russian winter.

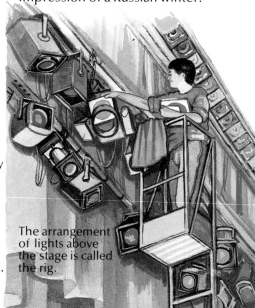

The arrangement of lights above the stage is called the rig.

*You can find out more about costumes on pages 18-19.

The publicity department

The marketing officer has posters printed to advertise a ballet. They are displayed where lots of people will see them, such as in libraries and stations, from four or five weeks before performances start. Advertisements are placed in newspapers and magazines.

Last rehearsals

From about two weeks before the first night (first performance), the dancers rehearse on stage to get used to its size. On the day before the first performance there is a full "dress rehearsal". Dancers wear their costumes and perform as if to an audience.

What happens backstage?

The cast must be backstage half an hour before the performance begins. First they put on their make-up.* Then they do their hair. A wig mistress helps to fit wigs and a dresser helps the cast into their costumes. The dancers put their ballet shoes on last. They may glue them to their tights to make them extra secure.

On stage

Stage manager

Wings →

The stage manager runs the show from a "prompt" corner.

Orchestra pit

Fifteen minutes before the performance, the orchestra take their place in the "pit" and tune their instruments.
   When the stage manager signals for the auditorium lights to go down, the orchestra begins the music and the stage manager gives the "curtain up" signal.
   The music is relayed to the dressing room, so dancers know when they are due on stage.

On tour

Most companies spend a good part of a year on tour in their own country and abroad. Their programme is worked out at least a year in advance.
   Everything travels with the company: costumes, scenery, lights and even office equipment.
   The ballet *La Fille Mal Gardée* has a small white pony in the cast. This would travel with the company along with its owner to care for it.

Everything is packed into huge lorries. Each dancer's make-up and practice costumes are stored in individual boxes, called "blue boxes".
   For a three month tour, about 30 pairs of satin *pointe* shoes are carried on tour for each female dancer and 18 pairs for each male dancer.
   The wardrobe staff take washing machines, tumble driers and crates containing sewing equipment.

*You can find out more about make-up over the page.

Costumes and make-up

Designing and making costumes is an art in itself. They help to create the mood of a ballet. As well as looking right, they must be light and easy to move in. Dancers often wear bits of old costume in rehearsals to help them get the feel of the ballet.

Hairstyles and make-up also help to conjure up weird and wonderful characters.

Different kinds of costume

Three different types of female costume reflect the Romantic, Classical and Modern movements in ballet. Fashion and social changes have had less effect on male costumes than on female costumes.

Classic costume.

Romantic costume.

The costume for a Romantic ballerina is a fairy-like, calf-length dress, usually white, with a fitted bodice and floaty sleeves. For fairy characters, wings may be attached to the shoulders.

The *tutu*, a short ballet dress with a tight bodice and layers of sticking out frills, is characteristic of Classical ballets.

Many Modern ballets are danced in simple, light dresses, or Greek-style tunics. All-over body tights are also worn by women and men. They are dyed and decorated in lots of different ways.

In Modern ballets, a dancer's hair may be worn in almost any style.It may be loose and natural or worn with a head-dress.

Male dancers usually wear tights. This is so the audience can see their legs executing the steps. In some Romantic and Classical ballets, men have to look like princes, so they wear tunics.

In Modern ballets, men's costumes are more varied. In the ballet *Enigma Variations,* the dancers wear ordinary trousers.

Character costumes

Many costumes help to portray a character. In *The Prodigal Son,* Balanchine's ballet of the parable from the Bible, the son wears a jewelled, Roman-style costume. This conveys his lavish spending and his rebellion against his Jewish family.

In the film ballet *The Tales of Beatrix Potter,* the dancers wear masks right over their heads to make them look like animals.

Some costumes express a theme or a spirit, such as the Spirit of the Rose in the ballet *Le Spectre de la Rose,* first danced by Nijinsky in 1911.

Prodigal son.

Mr Jeremy Fisher in *The Tales of Beatrix Potter.*

The Spirit of the Rose.

Making costumes

Costume designers make detailed sketches of their ideas. Sometimes they attach samples of possible fabrics. They have to remember that bright stage lights may distort colours and textures.

Jewellery is made of light, fake materials which gleam under the spotlights.

Mouse costume.

The costumes are made by skilled dressmakers and tailors. *Tutus* are especially hard to make.

Costumes must never restrict the dancers, so sleeves have to allow the arms to move freely. Fastenings consist of hooks and eyes instead of zips, so the dancers feel secure in them.

A *tutu* takes at least two days to make.

Make-up

Make-up is worn to accentuate the dancers' features so their faces can be seen under strong stage lighting. Eyes especially need to be highlighted.

Close up, stage make-up looks overdone. When seen by the audience it looks perfectly natural.

Make-up can also be used to create a character, such as a clown. Dancers use "nose-putty" to make false noses and chins. Careful highlighting can change the shape of a face and alter eyebrow shapes. Lines and smudges are painted on to look like wrinkles.

These pictures show a male dancer transforming himself into one of the Ugly Sisters in the ballet *Cinderella*.

1. A false plastic nose is glued on with special gum called spirit gum. ▶

2. Make-up exaggerates ▼ the lips and eyes and creates haughty, arched eyebrows.

Period costumes

Costumes may be designed to suggest a particular period in history.

Costumes for *Romeo and Juliet* were like 16th century Renaissance clothes to fit in with the period in which the story is set.

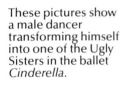

◀ 3. Sticks of greasepaint (special stage make-up) are used to shade and highlight the face, creating wrinkles and warts.

Making expressions

These expressions can be created by making up the eyes in different ways.

Mournful

Eyebrows and outer corners of eyes slope down. Dots at inner corners are put high up.

Fierce

Eyebrows are thickened and tilted up. Shading at the sides makes eyes look smaller. Wrinkles are painted between eyebrows.

Mild, simple

Eyebrows are arched and eyes enlarged.

19

Watching a ballet

Before you go to see a ballet, find out as much as you can about it. For instance, you could borrow a record of the music from a record library.

Buy a programme before the performance. This sets out the ballet's story or theme.

You can buy tickets from the theatre's box office or you can ask to be put on their mailing list. They will then send you details of future events. You return a form with money for ballets you want to see.

The *corps de ballet*.

In many Modern ballets the dancers make unusual shapes, like this.

Story ballets unfold with a mixture of dance and mime (see opposite). In some ballets the story is interrupted by set pieces of choreography when two or three people perform together. The *corps de ballet* dance together in group formations.

Ballets without a definite story have meaning, too. The dancers use all sorts of shapes and movements to express moods and reactions. If you look carefully, you may be able to understand what the dancers are saying with their bodies.

Steps to look out for

Here are some of the most difficult and exciting steps to look out for when you go to see a ballet.

Watch for changes in the speed of dancing, too.

Slow, gentle sections follow fast, vigorous ones. Group dances may follow solos. Sections are repeated or changed slightly to form a pattern.

Barrel turn

The barrel turn is also known as a *coupe jeté en tournant*.

Fish dive

Bourrées

Temps de poisson

The barrel turn, usually performed by a man, is a spectacular curving jump, followed by a quick turn on the ground. Some Russian dancers lean over so far that they are almost parallel with the floor.

A fish dive is performed by a male and female dancer. The male dancer catches the ballerina on his thigh as she swoops to the floor in a graceful, curving shape, like a fish darting through water.

Bourrées are performed *en pointe*. The dancer makes a series of tiny opening and closing steps. This gives the impression of gliding. It enables the dancer to travel across the stage very quickly.

The *temps de poisson* (fish step) is another fishlike movement. The dancer jumps in the air arching his body sideways like a sinuous, leaping fish.

This step is rarely performed by women.

20

Mime

Mime is a set of gestures which have a particular meaning and so help to tell a story. Some gestures are like the ones deaf people use.

In ballet there are over 200 mime gestures. They occur mostly in older ballets, such as *The Nutcracker*. However, the character Lise performs a mime in the Modern ballet, *La Fille Mal Gardée*. Here are some mime gestures you can look out for.

Beg

Incline your body forward, right arm outstretched and left arm slightly in front.

Love

Cradle your heart with both hands and incline your head slightly towards the left.

Plead

Place the palms of both hands together as if in prayer and incline your body forward.

Protect

Throw both arms back and hold your head high. Your body should face the danger.

You

Point your right hand towards the character concerned and face him or her.

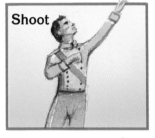

Shoot

Raise your arms and hands as if using a bow and arrow and look upwards.

Death

Extend your hands and arms and cross them in front of your body, with fists lightly clenched.

Fear

Turn away from danger, raise left arm over your head and shield your face with right palm.

Famous theatres and companies

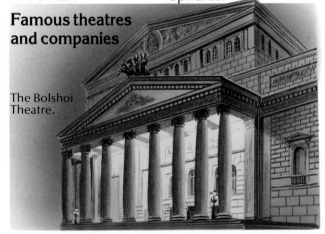

The Bolshoi Theatre.

Most dancers dream of performing in theatres such as the Royal Opera House in London, the Bolshoi Theatre in Moscow, the Metropolitan Opera House in New York and the Sydney Opera House.

Nowadays most major ballet companies travel abroad to dance in each other's theatres. This gives people in many countries the opportunity of seeing famous companies from all over the world.*

Choosing your seat

The best seats are usually in the centre of the auditorium and are slightly raised so you can see the dancers clearly. At the very front it is difficult to see the dancers' feet. The cheapest seats are usually high up in the gallery. From here you get a good overall view of the patterns the dancers make.

Some theatres run clubs for young people to join. Members can attend rehearsals and meet dancers.

*You can find out about some famous ballet companies on page 46.

Ballet as a career

Ballet can be an exciting and glamorous career but it is difficult to get into.

It is also a short career. The demands ballet makes upon the body mean that in their mid-30s most dancers have to take up other careers. Some become ballet teachers or critics.* Others become make-up artists or stage managers or retrain for totally different careers, such as accountancy.

Qualities you need

Well-shaped head.

Long neck.

Slim.

Neither too tall nor too small.

Well proportioned.

Strong arches neither too flat nor too high.

Strong feet.

As well as a good physique, a ballet dancer needs a sense of rhythm, a feeling for music, a good memory, an ability to accept correction and determination to work hard. Another important quality is a desire to bring pleasure to an audience.

Ballet training

You can start proper ballet classes at the age of seven. At ten or eleven, talented students may go to a full-time ballet school.**

Many promising students continue at an ordinary school until they are 16 or 17, taking ballet classes in their spare time.

Exam pass certificate.

An alternative is to go to a vocational school. Students get a broad theatrical training including acting, mime, ballet, modern dance, tap and folk dance as well as a general education.

Wherever you train you can take exams to mark your progress.

Further training

At about the age of 15 you will probably decide whether you want to become a professional ballet dancer, follow another career in the theatre or just continue ballet for fun.

If you want to become a professional ballet dancer you must train for at least two years at a full-time ballet school attached to a company. Such schools take students from the ages of 15 or 16.

Boy learning a sailor's dance.

As well as practising the basics, you learn how to dance with a partner and how to dance character roles. You learn some contemporary and folk dance and pieces from ballets to perform at auditions and to prepare you for joining a company. This helps build the confidence you need for a professional career.

Most ballet schools, for instance the Royal Ballet School in London or the New York Ballet School, are attached to a company. This means the company has a constant supply of new talent.

This also gives the students the chance to perform in small walk-on roles or in the back row of the *corps de ballet*. The professional experience is valuable for the students' careers.

*A ballet critic is somone who reviews ballets in books and newspapers.
   **You can find out about life at a ballet school on pages 24-25.

Joining a company

At the end of the training, a graduation performance takes place. The director of the company attends and picks out the most promising dancers to join the company.

The company may need to fill a vacancy during the year. The director watches classes and selects a dancer, usually after consultation with the ballet master or mistress.

If you do not manage to get into a major company you can apply to smaller companies at home or companies abroad. Write round asking to be seen and then audition until you get a job.

Alternative careers

You may have to give up the idea of being a classical ballet dancer, perhaps because you have not got all the specific qualities ballet demands. It could also be because you have grown too much or had an injury.

Whatever the reason, you may want to look for an alternative career.

One possibility for people who love performing is to work in the theatre. Some ballet dancers find they prefer this. For instance, the English dancer, Wayne Sleep, has moved from ballet to acting and singing.

Becoming part of the dance scene in the theatrical world is very different from joining a ballet company. The dancers must audition for every job and be able to dance in many different styles, including tap and jazz.

There are also opportunities in theatre and dance companies for those who wish to pursue theatre design, choreography and directing.

Another possibility is to change to contemporary dance. Many classically trained dancers prefer to work in this less rigid style. It is also useful because dancers do not have to conform to a stereotyped shape.

Ex-ballet dancer teaching choreology.

Many dancers turn to teaching at some stage in their career. They might teach in a full-time ballet school or start their own ballet classes.

If you decide early on that you want to teach, some ballet schools train people specially to teach ballet and dance. You can take exams to become a qualified ballet teacher.

Academic training

Nowadays you can study ballet and dance at polytechnics or universities. These courses cover the theory and history of dance as well as giving practical dance or ballet tuition.

With this sort of qualification you can teach ballet and dance in ordinary schools or the community.

It is unusual to join a ballet company after such a course, though some people join a contemporary company.

Life at a ballet school

If you show promise and have the right physique, you may begin full-time ballet school at the age of 11. Students come from all over the country and some from abroad, so many of them board at the school.

Despite the hard work and discipline expected of ballet students, competition to get a place is stiff and the selection procedure is tough.

Getting into ballet school

You can apply for an audition at the age of 11 even if you have never been to a ballet class. What is important is your physique and ability to express yourself in dance.

A group of examiners will watch you do simple exercises. They may ask you to make up a dance to music, to test the power of your imagination.

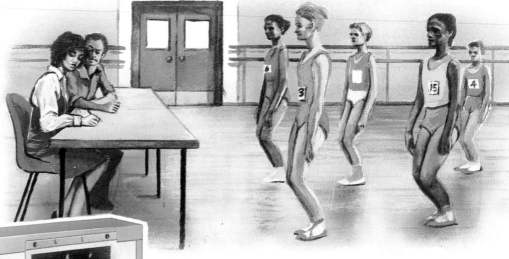

You will also be given a medical examination to check your fitness. In order to find out how much you are likely to grow, your hands are X-rayed. Girls must not grow too tall and boys must not be too small, as in classical ballet boys need to be taller than their partners.

The width of the dark gaps between the bones of the wrist show how much growth is ahead. The hand on the left has wide gaps which means a lot of growth is ahead.

Ballet classes

At first you spend about one and a half hours doing ballet. This increases as you move up the school. The classes are small and boys and girls are taught separately.

To begin with you concentrate on technique. As placing the parts of the body becomes automatic, you learn short dances, or *enchaînements,* at the end of the class.

When girls are 11 or 12 they start to go up *en pointe*. At first this is only done for a few minutes at the end of every class.

Gradually, more time is spent *en pointe* so after two years pupils do about an hour's *pointe* work a day.

You should not go *en pointe* until your teacher thinks you are ready. There is more about *pointe* work on page 39.

Boys' training is quite athletic. They use weights to build strength. When they have done this for at least a year, they take classes with girls, learning to partner but not yet lift them.

Theatre craft and choreography

Dancers wearing special character costumes.

Alongside ballet technique, other important aspects of ballet are taught, such as theatre craft. This tells you how to project yourself to an audience and convey different moods and emotions.

Students learn character dances from ballets and some folk and national dances. They wear special shoes for character dancing.

The students also have choreography classes. They may create their own dances or experiment with steps, putting them together to make interesting patterns.

Sometimes they may choose a particular theme and make up a dance to reflect it.

Choreology

Another skill you learn is choreology (see pages 12-13). You may use it in class for learning the steps of dances.

Other classes

As well as ballet classes, students do ordinary lessons. Some subjects, such as music, French and biology are stressed. Human biology helps students understand the skeleton and how muscles work.

Assessments

Each student's progress is regularly checked. These checks are called assessments. Pupils may be asked to leave the school if their dancing is not quite good enough or if they have grown too much or too little. As few students ever reach the top in ballet, they are always taught to look positively at alternatives to ballet.

Training round the world

Russia

The Kirov Ballet in Leningrad and the Bolshoi Ballet in Moscow have their own schools. Russian training is famous for teaching dancers to use their backs expressively, for instance, when doing spectacular leaps.

Denmark

The Royal Danish Ballet School is famous for a style established by a teacher called Auguste Bournonville. This style enables dancers to jump in a particularly bouncy way and is renowned for its neat footwork.

France

The Paris Opéra School is attached to the Opéra Company where many great dancers have made their début. Students are called *les petits rats* (the little rats)!

America

Training at the New York City Ballet School follows the style established by the founder of the company, George Balanchine. The style is swift and dramatic.

Britain

London's Royal Ballet School was originally started to supply new talent to the Royal Ballet Company. Today its pupils go on to dance with companies all over the world, as well as with the Royal Ballet.

Canada and Australia

Both the Canadian National Ballet and the Australian Ballet were founded by former members of London's Royal Ballet. Training is similar to that in Britain, though the National School in Toronto has developed a particularly lively style of ballet.

25

Exercises at the *barre*

On the next few pages there are some simple exercises for you to try. All the exercises follow the Cecchetti technique (see page 7). You might do them at a class and you can practise them at home.

On these two pages are some *barre* exercises. At home you can hold on to the back of a chair. At the *barre*, you usually practise an exercise in one direction and then turn round and practise facing the other way. This exercises both sides of your body equally.

Make sure that you always hold your spine and head very straight.

The elbow of your free arm must not droop. Hold your fingers gracefully. There are five positions of the arms. You can find out what they are on the opposite page.

Your toes on the floor should be long and straight. If you stand incorrectly your toes will curl up in order to grip the floor.

How far you stand from the *barre* is very important because it affects how you place your body. The hand on the *barre* should be slightly in front of your body and you should be able to imagine a straight line running down the middle of you.

If you stand too far away from or too close to the *barre*, this imaginary line will be distorted. Experiment to find the best position for you.

Pliés

*Pliés** are a good warming up exercise because they stretch all the muscles of your legs and prepare them for the later exercises. They also help you to achieve good turn-out.

There are two types of *pliés: grands pliés* (full knee bends) and *demi-pliés* (half knee bends).

Demi-pliés are especially good for stretching the tendons at the backs of your heels.

You can do *pliés* in all five positions of the feet (see pages 6-7). At first, practise them facing the *barre* with your feet in first and second position.

Demi-pliés

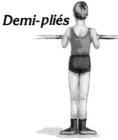

To do a *demi-plié*, face the *barre*. Rest both hands on it and put your feet in first position.

Grands pliés

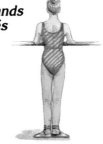

With *grands pliés*, you start in the same position as a *demi-plié*, with your feet in first position.

Battements tendus

Battements tendus literally means stretched beatings. They stretch and strengthen the arch underneath your foot.

In this exercise you point your foot to the front, side, back and side again. The pictures show the exercise to the front and side.

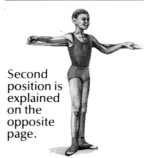

Second position is explained on the opposite page.

Put your feet in first position with your legs well turned out and your arm in second position.

Battements glissés

Glissé comes from the French verb *glisser* and means gliding.

In this exercise you slide your foot along the ground and lift it. It helps to develop swift footwork. You do this exercise to the front, side, back and to the side again. Here it is done to the side.

Put your feet in first position and place your arm in fifth *en bas* (see next page).

When you go down, don't "sit" on your hips. Lift up out of them when you rise up.

Bend your knees as far as they will go without letting your heels come off the floor.

Slowly straighten your knees, taking the same amount of time to rise as you took to go down.

Demi-plié in second position.

In a *demi-plié* in second position, you should feel the weight between your feet, not on your feet.

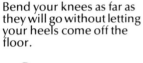

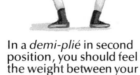

Do not pull on the *barre*.

Grand plié in second position.

Bend your knees, keeping your heels on the floor until you have to let them lift smoothly off it.

Now begin to rise slowly, first replacing your heels on the floor and then straightening your knees.

To do a *grand plié* in second, you must not lift your heels. Keep them firmly on the floor.

Point your toe and turn your leg out.

Stretch your right leg in front to fourth position. Then slide your foot back to close in first postion.

Now stretch your right leg to the side to second position. Keep your body and hips straight.

Bring your right leg back to first position. Repeat the exercise to the back and to the side again.

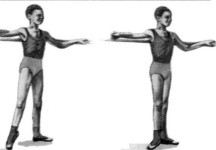

Do this to the front, side, back and side again.

Slide your foot along the ground to second. Lift it 5-7cm (2-3in) off the ground with toes pointed.

Now lower the toes to the floor to second position. Remember not to let your hips twist to the side.

Finally, slide your toes along the floor back to first position, gradually replacing your heel.

The positions of the arms

These positions follow the Cecchetti technique. They are the basic positions, though later on you will use your arms in many different ways.

First position

Second position

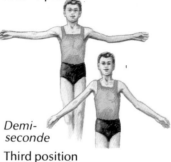

Demi-seconde

Third position

Fourth position

En haut

En avant

Fifth position

En haut

En bas

En avant

Rondes de jambe à terre

Here are some more exercises at the *barre*, starting with *rondes de jambe à terre*. This means circles of the leg on the ground. You mark out a semi-circle with your foot. It is an excellent way to loosen up your hip ligaments and improve turn-out. When you start the semi-circle at the front, it is called *en dehors*. When you start it at the back it is called *en dedans*. The pictures on the right show a *ronde de jambe en dehors*.

The exercises on these two pages are shown using the right foot. When you do them, repeat them with your left foot. There are some hints on pointing and positioning your feet on the far right.

Put your feet in first position and your right arm in second position.

Slide your right foot forward to fourth, pointing your toes. ▶

Battements frappés

Frappé comes from the French verb *frapper* which means to strike. In *battements frappés*, you cross your heel alternately in front and behind your supporting leg and strike the floor with your foot. This exercise should be performed with quick movements and is very good for sharpening your responses. It is a good preparation for jumping steps later.

A similar step to try is called *petits battements sur le cou-de-pied*. You can find out how to do it at the end of the row of pictures on the right.

Arm in second position.

Right heel resting on ankle bone.

Bend your right knee and cross your heel in front of your left anklebone. This is the starting position.

Sharply move your right foot down and out so the ball of your foot strikes the floor at the side. ▶

Grands battements

Grands battements means large beats. You raise your pointed foot from the ground, keeping both legs straight. This strengthens the legs and increases your extension (how high you can stretch them).

Like all other exercises at the *barre* you can perform *grands battements* to the front, side, back and to the side again. This is called *en croix*, meaning in the shape of a cross. These pictures show a *grand battement* to the front. You can do them with your feet starting in and returning to either first or fifth position.

Place your feet in first position and your right arm in second.

Point your right foot in front of you in fourth position. ▶

Développés

The name of this exercise means, as it sounds, developments. *Développés* are slow movements in which the leg is slowly extended to the highest point possible. The pictures on the right show a *développé* to the front. When you practise them, do them *en croix*, that is, to the front, side, back and to the side again.

Développés help you to learn control of your leg as it unfolds and to produce a beautiful line with your body. The movement should be done gradually and smoothly.

Stand up straight with your knees pulled up tightly.

Put your feet in fifth position and your right arm in fifth *en bas* (see previous page).

Point your right foot and gradually slide it up your leg to your knee. Keep both legs turned out. ▶

Do not twist your hips. Keep them level throughout the exercise.

Then slide your toes around on the floor to point to second position.

Next, slide your toes round to point to fourth position at the back.

Finally, slide your foot along the floor back to first position.

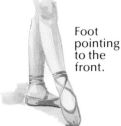

Foot pointing to the front.

Tips on pointing your feet

When you point your foot to the front, your leg should be turned out from the hip. Your heel should be held up, with the big toe touching the ground, not the little one. Your foot should be in line with your leg straight in front of you.

Your toes should be about 7cm (3in) off the ground.

When your foot leaves the floor after the strike, point it. At the same time tighten your knee.

Bend your right knee again and bring your right heel to the back of your left anklebone.

Petits battements sur le cou-de-pied

The name of this step means little beats on the ankle.

You alternately cross your outside heel in front and behind your inside ankle bone. Keep the ball of your foot on the floor and your foot flexed (not pointed).

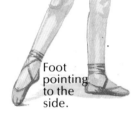

Foot pointing to the side.

When you point to the side, again make sure your foot is in line with your leg. Lift the heel and point the tips of your toes. Rest them only very lightly on the ground. Don't twist your heel backwards.

Keep your inside leg straight with your knee pulled tight.

Then lift your right leg as high as possible, keeping both your hips in line.

Next, lower your right foot to the floor back to fourth position.

Finally, slide your right foot back to first without bending your knee.

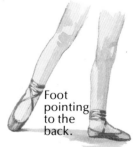

Foot pointing to the back.

At the back, rest lightly on the inside of your big toe and press your heel down. Don't turn your foot in as this will make your heel stick up in the air.

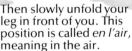

En l'air

As you slide your pointed foot towards your knee, smoothly raise your right arm in front of you.

Then slowly unfold your leg in front of you. This position is called *en l'air*, meaning in the air.

Straighten your leg out fully. At the same time, open your arm out to second position.

Centre work

In the second half of a ballet class you move away from the *barre* into the centre of the room. Here you repeat some of the exercises you have already done but without the *barre* to aid your balance.

Then you move on to specific centre work such as exercises for *port de bras* - the way you move your arms smoothly from one position to another. You also learn how to do steps such as the *arabesque* (shown opposite) and *allegro* (quick) steps. There are some *allegro* steps for you to try over the page.

In centre work there are eight basic positions you can use which show off the line of your body to best advantage from different angles. You can find out what they are below.

The eight positions of the body

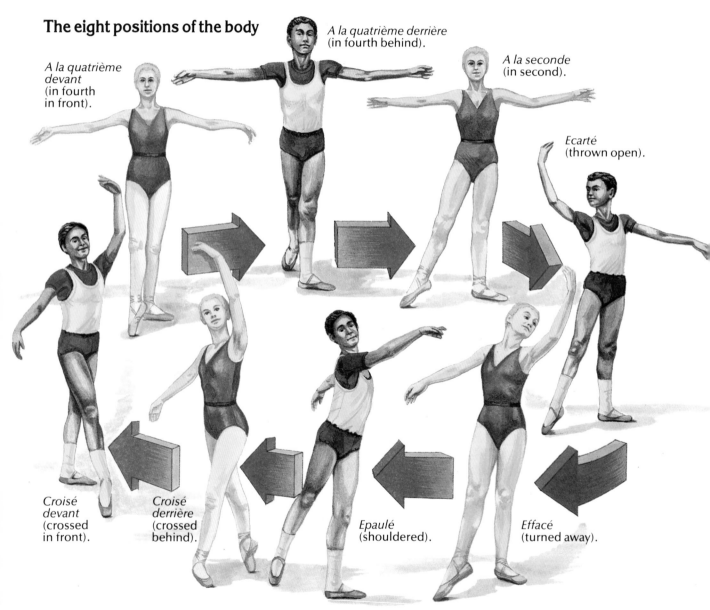

A la quatrième derrière (in fourth behind).

A la seconde (in second).

A la quatrième devant (in fourth in front).

Ecarté (thrown open).

Croisé devant (crossed in front).

Croisé derrière (crossed behind).

Epaulé (shouldered).

Effacé (turned away).

The eight positions or directions of the body form the basis of many of the movements in ballet. You will use them every time you do exercises in the centre. They are designed so that the audience see a clear outline of your body whatever direction you are facing.

Try out the eight positions yourself. The name of each position is shown next to it with its English translation in brackets.

Ports de bras

Ports de bras means carriage of the arms. They are exercises which teach you to move your arms in a graceful, flowing way.

Try the simple arm exercises on the right. Before you start, make sure you are standing up straight with your shoulders down.

Relax your arms, with the elbows and wrists slightly bent so your arms make a smooth curve. Your fingers should feel long and extended, but not tense.

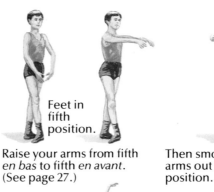

Feet in fifth position.

Raise your arms from fifth *en bas* to fifth *en avant*. (See page 27.)

Then smoothly open your arms out wide to second position.

Now take your arms back down through first position to fifth *en bas*.

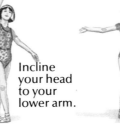

Feet and arms in fifth.

Incline your head to your lower arm.

Raise your right arm to fifth *en avant* and your left arm to *demi-seconde*.

Incline your head to your lower arm.

Swap the position of your arms passing them through second position.

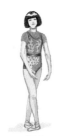

Lower both arms to fifth *en bas* passing the left arm through *demi-seconde*.

Arabesques

An *arabesque* is a well-known ballet position. It looks quite easy but it is difficult to do because it needs considerable control and balance.

You balance on one leg with your other leg stretched out behind you. Your arms can be in various positions but they must make a shape which compliments the position of the legs.

The pictures show you how to reach first *arabesque* through *développé à la seconde* and then how to move from first to second *arabesque*.

Arms in fifth *en bas*.

Raise arms to fifth *en avant*.

Stand with your feet in fifth. Gradually bend your right leg to the side.

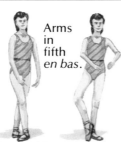

Pointing your right foot, slide it to your left knee and unfold your leg.

Open arms out to second.

Now extend your right leg out to the side (*à la seconde*).

Turn palms downwards and extend the fingers.

Turn your body sideways so your right leg is behind you. Turn both feet out.

Left heel slightly forward.

This is the first *arabesque* position.

Raise your left hand to eye level and slightly lower your right arm.

This is the second *arabesque* position.

Now swap the position of your arms, passing them through second position.

Adage steps

Slow, sustained movements such as the *arabesque* are called *adage* steps. *Adage* comes from the Italian *ad agio* meaning at ease.

When you do *adage* steps you should concentrate on developing grace, balance and "line". Line refers to the flowing curves which

your body makes. These smooth, graceful lines are characteristic of the harmony and balance of classical ballet.

Another common *adage* step is the *attitude*. In this step, you raise your leg behind your body, curving it by bending and lifting the knee.

Glissades

Glissades are gliding steps. You travel sideways by sliding your feet along the ground to your right, left, forwards or backwards. Make them as smooth as possible.

Start slowly and build up speed as you find them easier.

Stand with your feet in fifth and your arms in fifth *en bas* (low).

Widen your arms to first position.

Demi-plié and then slide your right foot along the ground.

Now raise your foot, pointed, to about 7cm (3in) above the ground.

▶

Pas de bourrées

In music, a *bourrée* is a dance done to a certain beat. In ballet, there are a variety of *bourrées*.

The step on the right is one of the first you will learn. It is called a *pas de bourrée en avant* (to the front).

You do this step facing the *effacé* direction. (This is explained on page 30.)

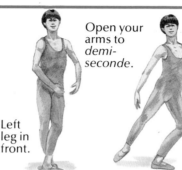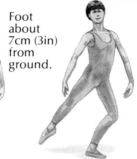

Left leg in front.

Open your arms to *demi-seconde*.

Foot about 7cm (3in) from ground.

Rising up on tip-toe is called *relevé*.

Face the *effacé* direction and place your feet and arms in fifth position.

Do a *demi-plié* on your left leg. Slide your right leg to the side and raise it.

Bring your right leg to close in fifth and rise up on tip-toe on both legs.

▶

Pirouettes

A *pirouette*, meaning a whirl, is a step where you spin on one leg. Here you can see how to do a *pirouette en dehors*. This is quite a simple step.

When turning, dancers use a special technique called "spotting" to prevent them getting giddy. You can find out more about it below.

Focus on a point straight ahead.

Stand with your feet in fifth position, left leg in front. Place your arms in fifth *en bas*.

Point your left leg to the side and pass your arms through fifth *en avant* to second positon.

Bend your right knee and bring your left heel to the back of your right ankle. Bring your arms to third.

▶

How to "spot"

Dancers have to learn how to "spot", that is, to focus on an object while turning or spinning in a *pirouette*.

In class, you learn to spot by looking at a fixed point on the wall. You focus on it for as long as possible during a turn before flicking your head round to look at it again.

Many theatres have a small, blue light especially for dancers on the stage to focus on. It is usually set very high up at the back of the auditorium.

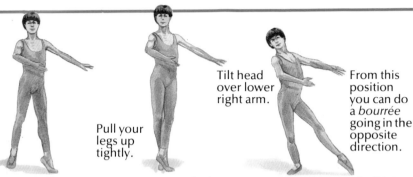

Bring your arms to *demi-seconde*.

Foot about 7cm (3in) above ground.

Glide as you transfer your weight to your right foot. Raise your left foot.

Incline your head to the right.

Arms in fifth *en bas*.

Now put your weight on your left leg and close your right leg in fifth.

Moving your head

When you do steps such as *glissades*, pay attention to the way you move your head.

In some positions, you incline your head to compliment the position of your body and aid your balance.

Allegro steps

Steps such as *glissades* and *pas de bourrées* are always done during the second part of centre practice. They are called *allegro* steps.

Allegro is an Italian musical term meaning quick and lively. This is how *glissades* and *pas de bourrées* should be performed.

However, practise them slowly at first until you get the hang of them.

When doing *allegro* steps make sure your arms do not flap about. Your aim should be to look as neat and controlled as possible without losing the vitality of the step.

Slide left leg forward on tip-toe and bring your arms to fourth *en avant*.

Pull your legs up tightly.

Bring your right foot to close behind your left foot, in fifth, *en relevé*.

Tilt head over lower right arm.

From this position you can do a *bourrée* going in the opposite direction.

Now do a *demi-plié* on your right leg and glide and raise your left leg.

Head turned over right shoulder.

Turn on the ball of the foot.

Bring your left leg to your right knee and turn on your right leg, lowering your arms to fifth *en bas*.

Flick your head round sharply when you have done a half-turn.

Continue the turn so your left knee faces the front and your head looks over your left shoulder.

Complete the turn and close your feet in fifth. Open your arms out to *demi-seconde*.

Turning steps

In ballet, a turning step is called a *pirouette*. There are many varieties of *pirouettes*. They can be done at any speed. Sometimes they form part of *adage** work. More usually they are done quickly and brilliantly as part of *allegro* work.

Ways to turn

There are two directions for a turn: *en dehors* (to the outside) and *en dedans* (to the inside). For a turn *en dehors* you turn away from your supporting leg. For example, if you are standing on your right leg, you lift your left leg and turn to the left.

Turning *en attitude*.

For a turn *en dedans*, you turn towards the supporting leg. For instance you stand on your right leg, lift the left leg and turn to the right. You can turn *en arabesque* (with your leg stretched behind you) or *en attitude* (with your leg curved round behind you).

**Adage* comes from the Italian musical term *adagio*, meaning slow.

Jumps and travelling steps

In the last part of a class you do jumps and travelling steps. There are two types: *petit allegro* (small and fast) and *grand allegro* (big and slower).

Jumps begin and end with a *demi-plié*. This helps you spring off the ground and land without jarring your joints.

When landing from a jump, the tips of your toes should touch the ground first. Your sole should touch the ground next and lastly your heel. This makes the landing smooth and quiet.

Changements

A *changement* is a jump in which you change the position of your feet before landing. Its name means changing. You can see how to do them on the right.

As you progress you may learn how to do *changements battus*, where you beat your legs together in the air before changing them.

Hold your arms in fifth *en bas*.

Don't hunch your shoulders or flap your arms.

Put your feet in fifth, right foot in front. Then *demi-plié*, keeping your heels on the ground.

Now jump straight up into the air with your legs straight and your toes pointed.

Change your legs in the air and land in a *demi-plié* in fifth position, this time with your left foot in front.

Entrechats

An *entrechat* is a step where you jump straight up in the air and change the position of your feet a number of times before landing. This is called "beating" your feet.

Entrechats are often combined with other steps and jumps.

On the right, you can find out how to do an *entrechat quatre*.

Arms in fifth *en bas*.

Keep your legs very slightly bent.

From a *demi-plié* in fifth position, right foot in front, spring into the air. As you jump, push your feet downwards.

While you are in the air, change the position of your legs very quickly so that your left leg is now in front of your right.

Before you land from the jump, change your legs back so you finish in a *demi-plié* in fifth, with your right leg in front.

Record breaking *entrechats*

The dancer Wayne Sleep has performed an *entrechat dix*, crossing and recrossing his legs five times before landing.

The Russian dancer Nijinsky is said to have done an *entrechat douze*, crossing his legs six times.

Wayne Sleep's achievement is in the Guinness Book of Records.

Pas de chats

A *pas de chat* (step of a cat) is a jumping step which is fun to do. Its movement is like a cat pouncing on a mouse.

You travel sideways through the air in a light, springing movement, often doing several in succession.

You can do them to your right or to your left. These pictures show you how to do them to your left.

Arms in third and head looking over curved arm.

From a *demi-plié* in fifth, right foot in front, jump to the left so the toes of the left leg are level with the knees of the right leg.

This is called the *retiré* position.

Now raise your right leg to meet the left leg in the *retiré* position and turn your head further round to the left.

Finally land in a *demi-plié* in fifth position with your right foot in front. You will be standing to the left of your starting position.

The Dance of the Cats

Pas de chat is used in the Dance of the Cats, in Act 3 of *The Sleeping Beauty*. It was created by the great choreographer of Classical ballets, Marius Petipa. He translated a cat's natural movements into classical ballet steps.

Assemblés

In an *assemblé* you jump with your feet apart and bring them together (assemble them) before you land.

It is a versatile step because it can be done to the front, back or side and can be a small or very large jump.

On the right you can find out how to do one of the simpler *assemblé* jumping steps.

Arms in fifth *en bas*.

Incline your head to your left.

Left leg in front.

Place your feet in fifth, with your right leg in front and do a *demi-plié*. Then slide your left foot to second and raise it.

As your left foot reaches second, spring off your right foot, into the air. Open your arms out to second.

Bring both feet together to meet in the air and land in a *demi-plié* in fifth position. Bring your arms back to fifth *en bas*.

Elevation

One of the aims of a classical ballet dancer is to jump lightly and travel gracefully. The ability to jump high and with ease is known as having good elevation. Usually men are expected to jump higher than women and to turn more times.

A simple dance

Here is a simple dance which you can practise at home. Before you try it, make sure you have plenty of room and are warmed up. The dance is mostly made up of steps described on the last few pages. The names of the steps are shown on the piece of paper on the far right. It ends with a new turning step called a *soutenu*.

Glissade derrière

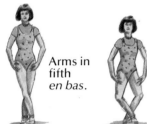

Arms in fifth *en bas*.

Incline your head to your left.

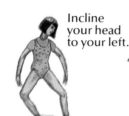

Place your feet in fifth position with your right foot in front and do a *demi-plié*.

Slide your left foot to second position and open your arms through first into *demi-seconde*.

As your arms reach *demi-seconde*, raise your left foot about 7cm (3in) and point it.

Then spring to the left. As you land, stretch your right foot off the ground, by about 7cm (3in). ▶

Two *changements*

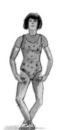

Keep your legs straight.

Straighten your legs and head, so you are looking directly to the front. Then do a *demi-plié*.

Now spring with straight legs into the air and swap the positions of your legs before landing.

Land in a *demi-plié* in fifth, right foot in front. Then spring into the air for the second *changement*.

Change your legs before landing, so you land with your left leg in front. Then straighten your legs. ▶

Soutenu

Open your arms out to second.

Lower your arms to fifth *en bas*. Make a small circle with the right leg, bringing it round your left leg.

This carries you into a turn to your left. Turn on the ball of your foot. Bring your feet to fifth position.

Continue the turn on tiptoe, moving your arms through fifth *en avant* up to fifth *en haut*.

End with your left foot in front, so you are ready to repeat the *enchainement*, this time to the right.

In ballet, steps like the ones in this simple dance are joined together like words to make a sentence. These sentences are called *enchaînements*, which means links. The steps are like the links in a chain.

A solo of variation in a ballet is made up of several *enchaînements* put together.

Glissade derrière
(to the left)
Assemblé dessus
(to the left)
Two changements
(on the spot)
Two pas de chats
(to the right)
Soutenu
(on the spot)

Assemblé dessus

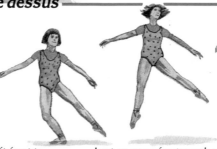

Bring arms to fifth *en bas*.

Slide your right foot back to a *demi-plié* in fifth. Lower your arms through first, to fifth *en bas*.

Slide your left foot to second, about 7cm (3in) off the ground. Open your arms to *demi-seconde*.

Just as your foot reaches second, spring in the air off your right foot. Lean your head to the left.

Bring both legs together in the air to meet and land gently in a *demi-plié*, with your left foot in front.

Two *pas de chats*

Arms in third.

Incline head to your right.

This is the *retiré* position.

From a *demi-plié*, jump to the right and bring the toes of your right leg to meet your left knee.

Raise your left leg to meet the toes of your right leg. Then land in a *demi-plié*, with the left leg in front.

Again, jump to the right, bringing the toes of your right leg to meet your left knee.

Raise your left leg to the *retiré* position. Land in a *demi-plié*, with your left leg in front.

Changing the Enchaînement

When you have practised the *enchaînement* a few times, try doing it at different speeds, as *petit* and *grand allegro*.

When this *enchaînement* is done quickly it has quite a different feel to it than when done slowly.

Once you have mastered the *enchaînement*, try to work out how to "beat" the *assemblé* and the *changements*. Beats are small, fast opening and closing movements of your legs, lightly beating your calves together in the air.

Steps for two

When a boy and girl dance together it is called *pas-de-deux* (steps for two). The *pas-de-deux* sections are the centre-pieces of most ballets. They usually express intense emotion such as love, grief or joy.

It takes years of practice and complete confidence in your partner to dance *pas-de-deux* well. Margot Fonteyn and Rudolf Nureyev were famous partners, as are Antoinette Sibley and Anthony Dowell.

Training for *pas-de-deux*

Pas-de-deux is usually taught in full-time ballet schools after the dancers have received a thorough training in all other aspects of ballet technique. The qualities required of the male and female dancer are different but equally demanding.

A boy must have the strength and control to lift the girl without overbalancing or dropping her.

Early training for boys includes weight-lifting to increase their strength. This is carefully regulated so that they do not develop bulky muscles which would spoil their streamlined appearance and slow them down.

Girls must be light but they also need strength, particularly in their wrists for hand grips. They also need strong feet and legs for dancing *en pointe* (see opposite).

Most of a girl's early training for *pas-de-deux* involves practice to develop her balance. The boy practices weight bearing exercises with the girl before moving on to the more difficult lifts and turns.

Developments in *pas-de-deux*

◀ This *pas-de-deux* from the Romantic era has a soft, dreamy look about it.

This *pas-de-deux* from ▶ a Classical ballet has more vitality than that of the Romantic ballet and the girl's leg is raised higher.

Modern ballets ▶ often bring partners into unexpected positions, like this one.

In the Romantic ballets of the mid-19th century, the ballerina was much more important than the male dancer. The men became known as *porteurs* (porters) because their job in a *pas-de-deux* was to carry the ballerina around.

Lifts were simple and the woman was mostly supported from behind.

In Classical ballets, *pas-de-deux* were made more dramatic and exciting.

Nowadays, due to Russian influence, lifts are more difficult and daring. Both partners take equal roles, though the male is always the support.

In many Modern ballets *pas-de-deux* is athletic and even gymnastic.

Dancing *en pointe*

Dancing *en pointe* means dancing on the tips of your toes.

The first ballerina to do this was Marie Taglioni, in the Romantic ballet *La Sylphide* (1832). She was trying to create the impression of a fairy-like creature, defying gravity.

It is important that you do not try to go *en pointe* until your ankles and feet are strong enough. Most girls are around 12 years old before they have enough strength to go *en pointe*. Do not try it without the guidance of a qualified teacher. Men very rarely dance *en pointe*.

One example, though, occurs in Frederick Ashton's ballet, *The Dream*. In this ballet, the character Bottom is magically turned into a donkey and dances *en pointe* to create the impression of an animal's hooves.

Pointe shoes

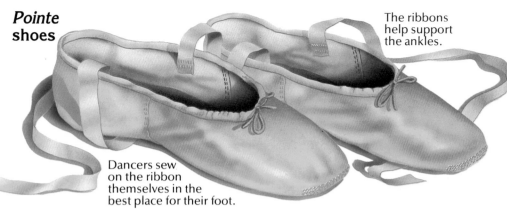

The ribbons help support the ankles.

Dancers sew on the ribbon themselves in the best place for their foot.

For dancing *en pointe* you need special satin slippers with stiffened toes. The toe part is made by "blocking" it with glue and baking it in an oven to harden and strengthen it.

Pointe shoes are very expensive because they are made by hand. The way they are made is kept secret by craftsmen who each have their own method.

A company dancer may get through up to ten pairs of *pointe* shoes a month. They do not wear out, but the glue softens and the shoes lose their support.

During a performance a ballerina may change shoes between scenes, using a softer pair for the *pas-de-deux* and harder pairs for *pirouettes* and hops *en pointe*.

Pointe technique

When dancing *en pointe*, lift your weight off your feet by keeping your knees straight and pulling up out of your hips. Your weight should be centred through your leg and foot.

The exercises below, called *relevés*, strengthen your feet, ankles and legs in preparation for *pointe* work.

Relevés

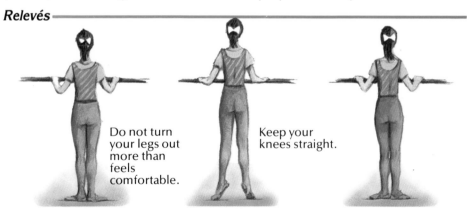

Do not turn your legs out more than feels comfortable.

Keep your knees straight.

Face the *barre*, resting both hands on it lightly. Turn your feet and legs out from the hips and pull your knees up tight.

Rise on to the balls of your feet and press them into the floor, making sure you can feel all your toes on the floor.

Then very slowly lower your heels back to the floor. Keep your legs straight and pull your knees tightly as you do so.

Problems with going *en pointe*

Going *en pointe* puts a lot of pressure on your toes and it does hurt. When you first start you may get blisters or your toes may bleed.

Experienced dancers only usually notice discomfort when they are standing still. However, many ballerinas develop bunions because the pressure forces the joint of their big toe out of line.

Famous choreographers

On these two pages you can find out about some famous choreographers and what influenced their work. The stories of some of the ballets they created are told on pages 42-43.

Choreographers fall into four main categories: Romantic, Classical, those of Diaghilev's company and Modern. Diaghilev's ideas paved the way for Modern ballet.

Romantic choreographers

Romanticism was a mood which influenced music, art and literature during the first half of the 19th century. People escaped from the depressing greyness of the Industrial Revolution into an imaginary world of faraway castles, spirits and the supernatural. The ballets created during this period reflect this interest in the supernatural.

Great importance was placed on the ballerina, whose gentle and passive image was idolized by a male-dominated, industrial society.

Scene from *La Sylphide*.

Although Paris was the centre of the ballet world at that time, two of the most famous choreographers were an Italian, Filippo Taglioni and a Danish ballet master, Bournonville, who later directed the Royal Danish Ballet.

While in Paris, Taglioni created *La Sylphide* in 1832 for his daughter, Marie, who typified the fairy-like, Romantic ballerina. In 1836, Bournonville created his own version of *La Sylphide* for a favourite pupil, Lucile Grahn.

Marie Taglioni

Jules Perrot

Jules Perrot was an important Romantic dancer and choreographer. He created the ballet *Giselle*.

Classical choreographers

Starting with Perrot in 1840, a succession of French choreographers went to Russia to work with the Imperial Russian Ballet in St Petersburg (now Leningrad). The company was financed by the Tsar and employed a composer to write music.

The extravagance of the Imperial Court is reflected in the Classical ballets created at this time. Their principle function was to display brilliant technique. The women dancers were therefore statuesque, rather than light and ethereal.

Perrot's first successor was St Leon who created *Coppélia*, to the music of Delibes. Then came the most famous Classical choreographer, Marius Petipa. With his colleague, Lev Ivanov and the composer Tchaikovsky, he created the great Classical ballets, *The Sleeping Beauty* (1890), *The Nutcracker* (1892) and *Swan Lake* (1895).

Petipa

Ivanov

Tchaikovsky

A costume for *The Nutcracker*.

The Classical ballets are made up of three or four acts and contain complex arrangements for the *corps de ballet* and *pas de deux*. A *pas de deux* is often followed by a male solo and then a female solo, created purely to show off the dancers' skill and technique.

Diaghilev choreographers

Petipa's successor at the Russian Ballet was Mikhail Fokine. He broke away from the formal structures of the earlier ballets. He made one-act ballets and used male dancers equally with ballerinas. In 1905 he created a solo, *The Dying Swan,* for Anna Pavlova.

Anna Pavlova

Fokine collaborated with a man called Diaghilev, whose brilliance lay in directing and co-ordinating the genius of others, whether they were dancers, choreographers, composers or designers. Between 1909 and 1929 Diaghilev's Russian Ballet, also known as the Ballet Russe, toured Europe revitalizing ballet and attracting new talent wherever it went.

Diaghilev had tremendous artistic vision, giving equal weight to dance, music and design. For example, under Diaghilev's guidance, Fokine joined forces with the composer Stravinsky and the designer Benois, to produce the ballet *Petrushka* in 1911.

Costume for Petrushka.

The changes of the 1910s, 20s and 30s, such as greater freedom for women, the jazz age, the First World War and the increased opportunity for sport and travel, are all reflected in Diaghilev's progressive ballets. The revolutionary impact of these changes can be seen in a ballet such as *L'Après-midi d'un Faune,* created by one of Diaghilev's protegés, Nijinsky. His ballet rejected every rule of turn-out and classical presentation of the body. This new style echoed the growing movement of contemporary dance.

Modern choreographers

After Diaghilev died in 1929, the members of his company spread their talents throughout Europe, Russia and America. George Balanchine, one of Diaghilev's stars, went to the USA to form the New York City Ballet. There he created a unique American classical ballet style with works such as *The Prodigal Son, Stars and Stripes* and *Serenade.*

Serge Lifar, Diaghilev's last male star, became director of the Paris Opéra Company, where he created such ballets as *Noir et Blanc.* Leonid Massine, also of the Ballet Russe, created roles in films such as *Red Shoes* which he did with Robert Helpmann.

In Britain, Marie Rambert started her own company, Ballet Rambert and Ninette de Valois founded the Sadler's Wells Theatre Ballet. This later became two companies, the Royal Ballet and Sadler's Wells Royal Ballet. De Valois encouraged young choreographers such as Kenneth MacMillan and John Cranko, who revitalized the Stuttgart Ballet in the 60s. She created her own works, too, such as *The Rake's Progress.*

Scene from *La Fille Mal Gardée.*

Two later directors of the Royal Ballet have created many works. Sir Frederick Ashton has made short ballets and full length works in the tradition of Petipa, for example, *La Fille Mal Gardée* and *Romeo and Juliet* for the Royal Danish Ballet. Kenneth MacMillan's dramatic works include *Mayerling* and *Manon.* He has prepared many of his ballets for staging by the American Ballet Theater.

Ballet today

Classical ballet continues to develop under choreographers such as David Bintley, who has created short and full length ballets, such as *Snow Queen,* for the Royal Ballet.

The Danish ballet star, Peter Schaufuss, now directs the London Festival Ballet, staging new works and directing revivals of older ballets.

In America, Glen Tetley continues to make exciting ballets, often combining classical ballet and modern dance. Another inspiring choreographer is Jiri Kylian of the Netherland's Dance Theatre. The National Ballet of Canada staged his ballet, *Transfigured Night,* in 1986. Constantin Patsalas, the National Ballet of Canada's own choreographer, has created almost 30 works, including the famous *Piano Concerto.*

Stories of ballets

Here is a selection of stories from Romantic, Classical and Modern ballets. There are also some ballets from the Diaghilev era. These came between Classical and Modern ballets.

Romantic ballets

La Sylphide

Choreography: Taglioni
Music: Scheitzhoeffner

James dreams of a fairy creature, the Sylphide, on the eve of his wedding to Effie. The Sylphide teasingly declares her love for him and snatches away Effie's ring. On the advice of a witch, James wraps the Sylphide in a scarf, to prevent her flying away. Her wings fall off and she dies. James is heartbroken, since by now his best friend has married Effie.

Giselle

Choreography: Coralli/Perrot
Music: Adam

Giselle loves Loys, whom she thinks is a poor country dweller, like herself. Loys is Count Albrecht. Giselle's fiancé, Hilarion, betrays Albrecht's secret. Giselle kills herself and joins the Wilis (spirits of girls who have died before their wedding night and seek revenge on men). They have killed Hilarion but Albrecht is saved from the same fate by Giselle's devotion.

Classical ballets

Coppélia

Choreography: St Leon and others.
Music: Delibes

Dr Coppélius makes a doll, Coppélia. Swanhilda's fiancé, Franz, falls in love with Coppélia and Dr Coppélius tries to bring her to life with a spell. Swanhilda pretends to be Coppélia, but Franz recognizes her. They are reunited.

The Nutcracker

The Nutcracker

Choreography: Ivanov
Music: Tchaikovsky

Clara is given a Nutcracker for Christmas. At night all her gifts come to life. Clara rescues the Nutcracker from a fight between toy soldiers and some mice. He takes her to the Kingdom of Sweets, where fairytale characters entertain her.

The Sleeping Beauty

Choreography: Petipa
Music: Tchaikovsky

In revenge for not being invited to Princess Aurora's christening, the wicked fairy Carabosse says Aurora will prick her finger and die on her 16th birthday. The Lilac Fairy lessens the spell by promising Aurora will fall asleep for 100 years and be woken by a prince's kiss. This happens and the Prince and Princess marry.

Swan Lake

Choreography: Petipa/Ivanov
Music: Tchaikovsky

While hunting, Prince Siegfried sees a swan, who changes into a young woman. She is Odette who has been turned into a swan by a wicked magician, Von Rothbart. The spell will only be broken if a man falls in love with her.

Von Rothbart presents his daughter, Odile, in the guise of Odette. Siegfried promises to love Odile and then realizes his mistake when a vision of Odette appears. Rothbart raises a storm on the lake and Odette kills herself. Siegfried follows her into the lake and the spell is broken.

Diaghilev ballets

The Dying Swan

Choreography: Fokine
Music: Saint-Saens

The Dying Swan is a solo dance, portraying the fluttering of a swan as it nears death. It was created for Anna Pavlova.

Firebird

Choreography: Fokine
Music: Stravinsky

Prince Ivan captures a Firebird. When he releases her, she gives him a magic feather to protect him. He later rescues a group of princesses, captured by the evil Kostchei and his monsters. Ivan marries the chief princess, Tsarevna.

Petrushka

Choreography: Fokine
Music: Stravinksy

A showman proves to his audience that his puppets (a Moor, a ballerina and Petrushka) come to life when he plays his flute. The crowd is horrified when Petrushka is killed in a fight with the Moor over the ballerina. The showman reminds them Petrushka is only a puppet. However, Petrushka's ghost rises to mock him.

Modern ballets

Le Spectre de la Rose

Choreography: Fokine
Music: Weber

A girl kisses the rose she has been wearing before dropping asleep. It falls to the floor and its spirit appears through the window. In the morning she remembers her dream but the rose has wilted.

Les Sylphides

The Sylphes

Choreography: Fokine
Music: Chopin (arr. Stravinsky)

This ballet has no real story. A young man, possibly a poet, dances with the spirits of young women (Sylphes). The ballet ends with the Sylphes encircling the poet, who is reluctant to leave.

L'Après-midi d'un Faune

Choreography: Nijinsky
Music: Debussy

A lonely faun is lying by a pool. He scares away all but one of a group of nymphs. She escapes when he becomes too friendly, but later creeps back to rescue a scarf she has dropped. She finds the faun comforting himself with the scarf, so she leaves him with his trophy.

The Rite of Spring

Choreography: Nijinsky
Music: Stravinsky

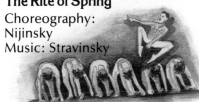

This ballet enacts a primitive ritual, celebrating the arrival of Spring. A girl is chosen as a human sacrifice by the elders. She has to dance till she falls dead from exhaustion.

Stars and Stripes

Choreography: Balanchine
Music: Sousa

Stars and Stripes conveys the spirit of the USA, with prancing drum majorettes and military drill. There are three groups of performers, dressed in patriotic costumes.

The Prodigal Son

Choreography: Balanchine
Music: Prokofiev

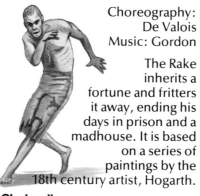

The Prodigal Son is based on a biblical parable. A son leaves home and joins a crowd of revellers, who rob him of everything. He drags himself home, fearing his father will not forgive him but he is welcomed.

The Rake's Progress

Choreography: De Valois
Music: Gordon

The Rake inherits a fortune and fritters it away, ending his days in prison and a madhouse. It is based on a series of paintings by the 18th century artist, Hogarth.

Cinderella

Choreography: Ashton and others
Music: Prokofiev

Cinderella is left at home while her stepsisters go to a Ball. A Fairy Godmother transforms Cinderella's rags into a ballgown and diamond slippers but warns her they will return to rags at midnight. At the Ball, the Prince falls in love with her. She runs away at midnight dropping a slipper. The Prince says he will marry whom the slipper fits. After a long search he finds Cinderella.

The Dream

Choreography: Ashton
Music: Mendelssohn

This is a one-act ballet of Shakespeare's play *A Midsummer Night's Dream*. It centres round an argument between Titania and Oberon over a mysterious Indian Boy, and the loves of Helena, Hermia, Demetrius and Lysander.

La Fille Mal Gardée

Farmyard scene from *La Fille Mal Gardée*.

Choreography: Ashton
Music: Hérold (arr. Lanchbery)

Lise loves Colas, a young farmer. Her mother, widow Simone, wants her to marry Alain, the clumsy son of a rich farmer. After many amusing adventures, widow Simone lets Lise marry Colas.

Romeo and Juliet

Choreography: Ashton, Macmillan and others
Music: Prokofiev

This ballet is based on a Shakespeare play. Romeo and Juliet come from feuding families. They fall in love and are secretly married, though Juliet is engaged to Paris. Romeo is banished after a fight. Juliet takes a sleeping potion to make her appear dead, so she will not have to marry Paris. Romeo thinks she is "dead" and kills himself. Juliet awakes, finds Romeo dead and kills herself.

Manon

Choreography: MacMillan
Music: Massenet

The ballet is based on an 18th century French novel about a young girl, Manon Lescaut, who is led astray by Parisian society. Chevalier des Grieux falls in love with her but Manon is deported to the swamps of Louisiana.

Famous dancers

These two pages tell you about some famous ballet dancers, past and present.

Barishnikov, Mikhail (born 1948)

Mikhail Barishnikov was born in Russia and studied at the Kirov Ballet School. He later left Russia to dance in the West.

He has danced with both the Royal Ballet, where he made his début in 1975 and the American Ballet Theater, where he became Director in 1980. He has danced both modern and classical works and appeared in several ballet films, including *The Turning Point* (1978) and *White Nights* (1986).

Bujones, Fernando (born 1955)

Fernando Bujones was born in Miami. He studied ballet in Cuba (his parents were Cuban), Miami and New York, and became a principal with the American Ballet Theater. He has made guest appearances all over the world, dancing a variety of roles, including ones created especially for him. In 1985 he danced at the White House for the American President and also made his début with the Royal Ballet.

Collier, Lesley (born 1947)

Lesley Collier was born in England and began dancing at the age of two. She went to the Royal Ballet School and joined the Company in 1965. She has danced roles in all the great classical ballets, including Juliet in Kenneth MacMillan's *Romeo and Juliet* (1973) and Lise in *La Fille Mal Gardée* (1970).

Sir Frederick Ashton created *Rhapsody* for Collier and Barishnikov for the English Queen Mother's 80th birthday in 1980.

Dolin, Anton (1904-1983)

Diaghilev spotted the English dancer, Anton Dolin (Patrick Kay) at the age of 19. This resulted in Dolin appearing in *The Sleeping Beauty* for the Ballet Russe.

In 1928 he began a famous partnership with Alicia Markova. They formed the Markova-Dolin Ballet Company in 1935. Later in life he turned increasingly to choreography and directing.

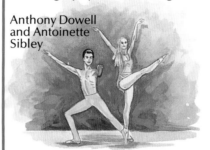

Anthony Dowell and Antoinette Sibley

Dowell, Anthony (born 1943)

London-born Anthony Dowell trained at the Royal Ballet School and joined the Company in 1962.

He danced Oberon in the first production of *The Dream* in 1964. This began his partnership with Antoinette Sibley.

He is especially good at bringing to life heroes such as Albrecht (*Giselle*), Prince Siegfried (*Swan Lake*) and Prince Florimund (*The Sleeping Beauty*).

He spent a year dancing with the American Ballet Theater in 1978 and became Director of the Royal Ballet in September 1986.

Eagling, Wayne (born 1950)

Wayne Eagling was born in Canada. He went to the Royal Ballet School in London and joined the Company in 1969.

In 1973, he danced Romeo for the first time with Lesley Collier. He has since danced leading roles in many major ballets.

In 1986 he created a new ballet, *Frankenstein*, with music by Vangelis and costumes by Emanuel.

Fonteyn, Margot (born 1919)

Margot Fonteyn studied at the Sadler's Wells Ballet School in London where she was singled out as a soloist at the age of 16.

She is well known for two long and famous partnerships. The first was with Michael Somes and the second was with Rudolf Nureyev after his defection from Russia in 1962. By then Sir Frederick Ashton had created many roles for her. Her partnership with Nureyev inspired still more.

Makarova, Natalia (born 1940)

Natalia Makarova is Russian. She trained at the Leningrad Ballet School and joined the Kirov Ballet in 1959. In 1970 she left the company while the Kirov were appearing in London and joined the American Ballet Theater.

There is a fragile quality to her dancing, which makes her excel in roles such as Giselle.

She appeared in the musical *On Your Toes* and is continuing her career in musical theatre.

Alicia Markova

Markova, Alicia (born 1910)

Alicia Markova joined Diaghilev's Ballet Russe at the age of 14 after Anton Dolin persuaded Diaghilev to watch her dance. Markova was Sadler's Wells' first prima ballerina. She formed the Markova-Dolin Company with Anton Dolin in 1935.

Mitchell, Arthur (born 1934)

Arthur Mitchell went to Balanchine's School of American Ballet. This was unusual as he is black and at that time there were no black classical ballet dancers. He later joined the New York City Ballet.

In 1969 he formed an all black company, the Dance Theater of Harlem, in response to the murder of the black civil rights leader Martin Luther King. His company is now internationally famous and performs all over the world.

Nijinsky, Vaslav (1890-1950)

Nijinsky's dancing career was short but spectacular. He joined the Russian Imperial Ballet School, then the Ballet Russe as Diaghilev's protegé. His most famous role was the Spirit of the Rose. He choreographed *L'Après-midi d'un Faune* (1912), followed by *The Rite of Spring* in 1913.

Nureyev, Rudolf (born 1938)

The Russian dancer Rudolf Nureyev began his training at the late age of 17.

While in Paris in 1961, he left the Kirov Ballet to dance in the West. The following year he made a spectacular début with the Royal Ballet in *Giselle*. This was the beginning of a legendary partnership with Margot Fonteyn, which inspired many new ballets.

Nureyev is now Director of the Paris Opéra Ballet and still makes guest appearances with companies all over the world.

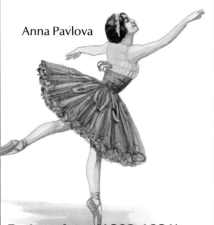

Anna Pavlova

Pavlova, Anna (1882-1931)

Anna Pavlova joined the Imperial Ballet School in St Petersburg (Leningrad) and danced all the principal roles in Petipa's ballets at the Maryinsky Theatre.

She later danced with the Ballet Russe and formed her own company.

She is most remembered for her solo, *The Dying Swan*.

Seymour, Lynn (born 1939)

Canadian-born Lynn Seymour trained at the Royal Ballet School in London. She joined the Royal Ballet Company in 1957, left to dance with the Deutsche Opera in 1966 and returned to the Royal Ballet in 1970.

Her dramatic dancing inspired MacMillan to create many roles for her, including Juliet.

She was guest artist with many companies and, before retiring, directed the Munich Ballet.

Schaufuss, Peter (born 1949)

Peter Schaufuss was born in Denmark, the son of Danish ballet' stars. Since leaving the Danish Ballet School he has danced with the National Ballet of Canada, the London Festival Ballet, the Kirov and Bolshoi Ballets, the New York City Ballet and others.

He is now an established artist, producer and choreographer with companies all over the world. He is currently Artistic Director of the London Festival Ballet.

Sibley, Antoinette (born 1939)

Antoinette Sibley is a British dancer. She trained at the Royal Ballet School and is a member of the Royal Ballet Company.

She is particularly famous for her interpretation of roles, especially Titania in *The Dream*, Dora Penny in *Enigma Variations* and the title role in Kenneth MacMillan's *Manon*.

Her famous partnership with Anthony Dowell began in 1964.

She played Sevilla in the film *The Turning Point*.

Wayne Sleep is very good in comic roles.

Sleep, Wayne (born 1948)

Wayne Sleep trained at the Royal Ballet School and joined the Company in 1966. His lack of height is an asset in certain roles such as Puck in *The Dream*. He was also one of the Two Bad Mice in the film *The Tales of Beatrix Potter*.

Sleep left classical ballet to pursue a career in musical theatre. He formed his own company, Dash, and appeared in a successful TV series, *The Hot Shoe Show* which he took on tour.

Taglioni, Marie (1804-1884)

Marie Taglioni was the first dancer to break away from tradition by dancing *en pointe*. She was trained mainly by her father, Filippo Taglioni. She created the title role in *La Sylphide*, the ballet which marked the birth of Romantic ballet.

Famous companies

Below you can find out about some of the world's most famous ballet companies.

America

New York City Ballet

When George Ballanchine founded the New York City Ballet in 1948, he had already created many ballets. He went on to develop a unique athletic style of classical ballet for which the company is renowned.

American Ballet Theater

The first performance by the American Ballet Theater was in 1940. The company stages a wide range of ballets, including Russian Classical ballets, the Diaghilev ballets and contemporary American works.

Dance Theater of Harlem

In 1971, Arthur Mitchell, a leading black dancer with the New York City Ballet, founded a ballet company in Harlem, the black quarter of New York. The company offers a part classical, part ethnic repetoire of ballets.

Australia

The Australian Ballet

The foundations of the Australian Ballet were laid by Edouard Borovanky, ex-member of Ballet Russe. His company formed the nucleus of the new Ballet, founded in 1962 by Dame Peggy van Praagh, formerly director of the Sadler's Wells Theatre Ballet.

Britain

The Royal Ballet

The Royal Ballet, originally the Vic-Wells company, was founded by Ninette de Valois.

In 1946 it moved from the Sadler's Wells Theatre to London's Royal Opera House, although a second company stayed to work at Sadler's Wells.

London Festival Ballet

After a successful tour of Britain in 1949, Alicia Markova and Anton Dolin formed the London Festival Ballet, named after the Festival of Britain. The company policy has always been to stage both old and new ballets.

Ballet Rambert

Ballet Rambert, named after its founder Marie Rambert, is the oldest of Britain's companies. In its infancy, it encouraged many fine dancers and choreographers. Today it successfully combines classical ballet and Modern dance.

Canada

The National Ballet of Canada

The National Ballet of Canada was founded by Celia Franca, a former member of the Royal Ballet. Although its style resembles that of the Royal Ballet, Modern-dance choreographers are increasingly involved.

Denmark

The Royal Danish Ballet

The ballets of Danish choreographer Bournonville (1804-1879), are still popular with the company's audiences, although nowadays it stages a wide variety of works often in stark contrast to Bournonville's style.

France

The Paris Opéra

In the 1930's the Paris Opéra was revived by one of Diaghilev's pupils, Serge Lifar, who created a large number of ballets for the company. Nowadays many of its ballets are created by guest choreographers, such as Glen Tetley and Merce Cunningham.

Germany

Stuttgart Ballet

When choreographer John Cranko joined the Stuttgart Ballet in 1961, his ballets, performed by an inspired group of dancers, brought the company international fame. Despite Cranko's death in 1973, the company still flourishes.

Holland

The Dutch National Ballet

The Dutch National Ballet was formed from two existing companies in 1961. It performs a wide variety of ballets.

Nederlands Dans Theater

Founded in 1959, the Nederlands Dans Theater is renowned for its staging of progressive ballets. Although strongly influenced by American choreography, its own distinctive character is emerging under Jiri Kylian.

Russia

Ballet Russe

Between 1909 and 1929 Diaghilev's Russian Ballet company revitalised ballet, staging works choreographed by Fokine and Nijinsky. Diaghilev also utilized the artistic and musical talents of great designers and composers.

The Bolshoi Ballet

After the Russian Revolution of 1917, Alexander Gorksy, a new teacher at the Bolshoi Ballet in Moscow, encouraged the dancing to be more colourful.

Today the company stages old ballets and new ballets, often expressing socialist ideas.

The Kirov Ballet

Today the Kirov Ballet is renowned for its nobility of style and for the expressive and fluid way dancers use their arms and backs.

Ballet words

A la quatrième derrière. In fourth position behind. (One of the eight **positions of the body** in **classical** ballet.)

A la quatrième devant. In fourth position in front. (One of the eight **positions of the body** in **classical** ballet.)

A la seconde. In second position. (One of the eight **positions of the body** in **classical** ballet.)

Adage. Slow, sustained movements.

Administrative director. The person responsible for a company's major policy decisions.

Alignment. The lining up of parts of your body to make a balanced and graceful outline.

Allegro. An Italian musical term meaning quick. In ballet, *allegro* steps are fast steps.

Arabesque. A position in which you balance on one leg with the other stretched out behind you.

Artistic director. The person in a company who decides which ballets will be performed and who will dance each role.

Assemblé. A travelling step in which you jump with feet apart and bring them together before landing.

Assessment. A check on a ballet student's progress.

Attitude. A position in which you stand on one leg and lift and curve the other leg round behind you.

Backcloth. A large cloth hanging down at the back of the stage on which scenery is painted.

Ballerina. A female dancer of **principal** or **soloist** status.

Ballet master or mistress. The person who rehearses ballets and supervises the *corps de ballet.*

Barre. A wooden hand rail that runs round the walls of a ballet **studio**. It is used to aid balance while doing exercises.

Barrel turn. A type of leap in which the dancer travels in a large circle.

Battement frappé. An exercise in which you cross your heel alternately in front and behind the ankle of your supporting leg, pointing your leg to the side between each position.

Battement glissé. An exercise in which you slide your foot along the ground and lift it.

Battement tendu. An exercise in which you stretch your foot along the floor to the front, side, back and side again (*en croix*).

Beating. Rapid, opening and closing movements of stretched legs during a jump.

Benesh notation. A system of dance **notation**. It was developed by Rudolf and Joan Benesh.

Bourées. A series of tiny steps which give the impression of gliding along the floor.

Call sheet. A rehearsal timetable for dancers in a company.

Cecchetti technique. One of the techniques of **classical** ballet.

Centre practice. Exercise done in the middle of the **studio** without the support of the *barre.*

Changement. A jump in which you take off with one leg in front and land with the other leg in front.

Changement battu. A *changement* in which you **beat** your legs before landing.

Choreographer. Someone who creates, or choreographs, ballets by putting steps to music.

Choreologist. Someone who writes dance steps down using **notation**.

Classical. A term used to describe ballet technique. Also used to describe ballets of the latter half of the 19th century which display classical ballet in its purest form.

Contemporary dance. A modern style of dance, less rigid in structure than **classical** ballet.

Corps de ballet. A large group of dancers in a ballet who perform the same steps.

Coryphée. A leader of the *corps de ballet* or a dance on the way to becoming a **soloist.**

Coupe jeté en tournant. See **Barrel turn**.

Croisé devant. Crossed in front. (One of the eight **positions of the body** in **classical** ballet.)

Croisée derrière. Crossed behind. (One of the eight **positions of the body** in **classical** ballet.)

Cross-over. A type of cardigan worn in class which crosses over at the front and ties at the back.

Curtain up. The start of a performance when the stage curtains rise.

Demi-plié. A half knee-bend.

Demi-pointe. Half point i.e. standing on the balls of your feet.

Demi-seconde. An arm position half way between first and second positions.

Développé. An exercise in which you slowly raise and unfold your leg.

Education officer. The person in a company who organizes contacts with schools and the community.

Effacé. Turned away. (One of the eight **positions of the body** in **classical** ballet.)

Elancer. To dart. One of the seven **movements of dance**.

Elevation. The ability to jump high, with ease.

En avant. Above. (One of the eight **positions of the body** in **classical** ballet.)

En bas. Below. A term used to describe the arms when held low.

En croix. In the shape of a cross. It describes exercises done to the front, side, back and side again.

En dedans. To the inside. It describes a turn towards the supporting leg.

En dehors. To the outside. It describes a turn away from the supporting leg.

En haut. High. A term used to describe the arms when held above the head.

En pointe. Standing or dancing on the tips of your toes.

En relevé. On the balls of your feet.

Enchaînement. A series of steps linked together to make a dance sequence.

Ensemble. A group formation of dancers in some **Modern** ballets.

Entrechat. A jump in which you take off with one foot in front, change your feet over and then change them back before landing.

Epaulé. Shouldered. (One of the eight **positions of the body** in **classical** ballet.)

First night. The opening performance of a ballet.

Fish dive. A step in which the man catches the woman as she swoops towards the ground in a fish-like movement.

Fish step. See *temps de poisson*.

Glissade. A travelling step in which you glide your foot along the ground and transfer your weight on to it.

Glisser. To glide. One of the seven **movements of dance**.

Graduation performance. A performance at the end of ballet students' training at which the most promising dancers are chosen to join the company.

Grand allegro. Large jumping and travelling steps.

Grand battement. An exercise in which you point your foot and raise it.

Grand jeté. A leap through the air with legs outstretched.

Grand plié. A full knee-bend.

Labanotation. A system of dance **notation**. It was devised by Rudolf von Laban.

Mime. A set of gestures each with a particular meaning which help to tell a story.

Modern. A term used to describe ballets created during the latter half of this century.

Movements of dance. Seven types of dance movement based on natural movements of the body.

Notation. Systems of signs used to record dance steps on paper.

Pas de bourrées. A travelling step done to a *bourrée*, or type of dance music.

Pas de chat. Step of a cat. A travelling step.

Pas-de-deux. Steps where a boy and girl partner each other.

Petit allegro. Small jumping and turning steps.

Petit battement sur le coup de pied. An exercise in which you alternately cross your heel in front and behind the ankle of your supporting leg.

Physiotherapist. A person trained to treat dancers' injuries.

Pigs' ears. The name given to untidy ends of ballet shoe ribbons that stick out after being tied.

Pirouette. A turning step, meaning a whirl.

Pit. Where the orchestra sit, below the front of the stage.

Placing. The position of one part of your body in relation to another.

Plié. A knee-bend.

Plier. To bend. One of the seven **movements of dance**.

Pointe shoes. Block-toed ballet shoes used for dancing **en pointe**.

Port de bras. Set movements of the arms from one position to another.

Positions of the body. Eight different ways of standing and holding your arms which show off the line of your body when doing **centre practice**.

Positions of the feet. Five different positions in which your weight is evenly distributed over your feet whatever position your body is in.

Premier danseur. A title which can be given to a **principal** male dancer.

Press officer. The person in a company who maintains contact with the Press, informing them of a company's future performances.

Principal. A dancer who performs a leading role in a ballet.

Relever. To rise. One of the seven **movements of dance**.

Relevé. An exercise in which you rise up on the balls of your feet.

Répétiteur. A person who rehearses ballets with the dancers.

Rig. The arrangement of stage lights.

Romantic. A term used to describe the style of ballet created during the Romantic era in the first half of the 19th century.

Rondes de jambes à terre. An exercise in which you mark out a semi-circle on the ground with your pointed foot.

Rosin. A yellow crystal which breaks down into a white powder. Dancers rub the soles of their shoes in it to stop them slipping.

Set. The scenery and props on the stage.

Soloist. A dancer who dances alone, or solo, in a ballet.

Soutenu. A turning step.

Spotting. A technique used by dancers to stop them becoming giddy when turning fast.

Stage manager. The person who co-ordinates the lighting, scene changes, dancers and so on during a performance of a ballet.

Stave. Five parallel lines on which music or dance **notation** can be written.

Studio. A room where ballet classes are held.

Technical director. The person in charge of the lighting, special effects and so on in a ballet.

Temps de poisson. A jump in which the dancer bends his body like a fish.

Theatre craft. The art of performing to an audience.

Tourner. To turn. One of the seven **movements of dance**.

Turn-out. The technique belonging to **classical** ballet of turning the legs out to the side from the hip sockets.

Tutu. A ballet costume with a fitted bodice and a short, sticking out skirt. Characteristic of **Classical** ballet.

Wardrobe. The costume department of a ballet company.

Warm-up. Simple exercises at the start of a class which prepare the muscles for more demanding movements.

·PART TWO·

DANCE

Lucy Smith

Edited by Helen Davies and Pam Beasant

Designed by Nerissa Davies

Contents

Dance Consultants: Jan Murray, Bronwyn Williams, Warren Hayes, Terry Monahan, Sue Davies, Patrick Duncan, Colin Holsgrove and Jeannette Mac Donald

Illustrated by Kathy James, Chris Lyon, Mick Posen, Sue Stitt, Cathy Wood, Nerissa Davies and Gordon Lawson

About dance

All over the world people have always danced. Dancing is a way of expressing moods and feelings by making shapes with your body and moving in a rhythmical way. In many countries, dance is an important part of the culture and special occasions are often accompanied by dancing.

In part two you can find out about lots of kinds of dance, including those shown below.

Contemporary dance

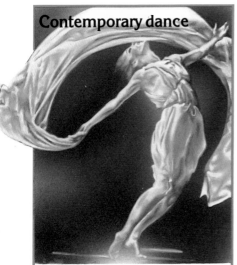

Contemporary dance began at the start of this century when Isadora Duncan broke away from ballet and invented a very individual style of dancing. Another American dancer, Martha Graham, developed a contemporary dance technique which is now taught in many classes.

Jazz dance

Jazz dance first developed with jazz music in the 1920s. In the 1950s, as popular music changed, so did jazz dance. Today there are many different styles of jazz, danced to various kinds of music. They all feature energetic and rhythmical movement. To do jazz you need to be fit and supple.

Tap dance

The movements of tap are concentrated in your feet. Wearing shoes with metal toe-caps, you tap out the rhythm of the music you are dancing to. To tap dance you do not have to be as fit as you do for some other kinds of dance, but you need to move in a flowing, graceful way.

Popular dances

Popular dances are done with other people and not necessarily to entertain an audience. Disco dancing, body popping, breakdancing and rock 'n' roll are all popular dances. You can find out more about them and learn some of their basic steps later in this part of the book.

Why dance?

There are lots of good reasons to dance. It gives you a healthier body, it makes you feel happy and confident and it can be very exciting to do. It is also great fun to dance with friends. You can dance to almost any music you like, as long as it has a good rhythm.

Learning to dance

There are classes in almost every kind of dance, and you can learn popular styles such as disco by watching other people. You do not have to be very fit to start dancing, nor do you need an expensive new wardrobe of clothes. All you need are clothes which let you move freely.

Learning to dance for fun does not take long, but if you want to be very good or professional you will need to devote a lot of time to it.

TIMETABLE
MONDAY

TIME	STYLE	LEVEL	HRS
9.30	JAZZ	BEGINNER	1
10.00	AMERICAN TAP	INTERMEDIATE	2
12.30	BALLET	INTERMEDIATE	2½
1.00	ROCK JAZZ	BEGINNER	1
2.00	CEROC	BEGINNER	1
3.00	FLAMENCO DANCING	ADVANCED	1½
4.00	CONTEMPORARY	INTERMEDIATE/ADVANCED	1½
5.00	BELLY DANCING	BEGINNER	1

About this book

In part two you can find out how the different types of dance began and developed and the famous dancers associated with them. You can learn about creating dances and about how music and dance go together. There are also some simple moves and steps for you to try yourself.

Classes

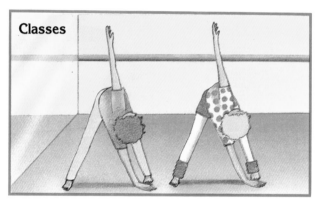

Part two explains what happens at a dance class and how to prepare your body for dance. There are hints on what to wear too.

Companies

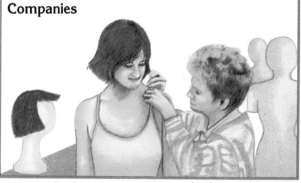

You can find out about dance companies and the different jobs people do, such as designing and making dancers' costumes.

Staging

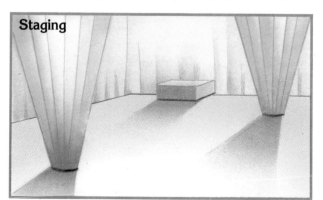

You can also see how a dance is prepared for the stage, or "staged", from designing the set to creating lighting effects.

Sport

Ice-skating and gymnastics are sports which use dance movements. You can find out about this at the end of part two.

Preparing to dance

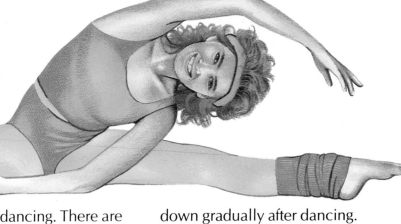

Dancing makes great demands on your body. Before you start any dance session, you should do some warm-up exercises. These are gentle exercises which help to loosen and stretch your muscles and prepare them for more vigorous work. If you do not warm up your body, you may damage a muscle while you are dancing. There are some warm-up exercises for you to try on pages 54-55.

It is also important to cool down gradually after dancing. This is to allow your muscles to recover and your pulse rate to return to normal.

What to wear

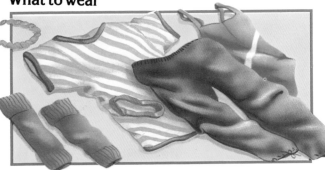

To warm up, you can wear any clothes that are comfortable and allow you to move freely. Clothes made from natural fibres are good because they are warmer and absorb sweat. It is best to warm up either in bare feet or soft dance slippers.

If you have long hair, tie it back. Remove any jewellery that is likely to get caught or that might scratch you.

Where and when to dance

Linoleum

A "sprung" floor is made of wooden boards which give when you jump on them.

Wooden boards resting on joists.

Ideally you should go to a class at a dance studio with a sprung wooden floor, varnished or covered with linoleum to prevent splinters. Never dance on very hard floors, such as concrete, as this jars your joints.

At home, exercise on a carpeted or smooth, clean floor. Try to wait two hours after a meal before dancing, or you may get stomach cramps.

Why muscles need warming up

The muscles used for moving are made up of long, thin strands of tissue known as muscle fibres. These fibres cannot replace themselves if they are damaged. Warm-up exercises stretch the muscle fibres slightly and prepare them for harder work.

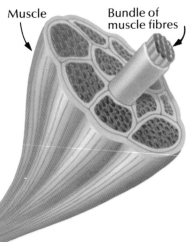

Muscle

Bundle of muscle fibres

Breathing

When you exercise you need to breathe using both the lower and the upper parts of your lungs. To check you are doing this place one hand on your stomach and the other on your chest. As you inhale, you should feel your stomach move first, then your chest.

Stomach moves first . . .

. . . then chest.

Checking your pulse

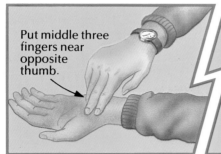

Put middle three fingers near opposite thumb.

HOW TO CALCULATE YOUR MAXIMUM PULSE RATE:

$$220 - (\text{YOUR AGE}) = \text{YOUR APPROXIMATE MAXIMUM PULSE RATE}$$

E.G. IF YOU ARE AGED 10:
$$220 - 10 = 210$$

TO CALCULATE 3/5 OF YOUR MAXIMUM PULSE RATE:

E.G. IF YOUR MAXIMUM PULSE RATE IS 210:

$$\frac{3}{5} \times 210 = \frac{3 \times 210}{5}$$
$$= \frac{630}{5} = 126$$

Your pulse shows the rate at which the blood is pumped round your body. To take your pulse you need a watch which shows seconds. Put the middle three fingers of one hand on the wrist of the other hand. Count how many times your pulse beats in fifteen seconds and multiply this by four.

To find out how well you are exercising you need to compare your pulse rate with your "maximum pulse rate". This is the highest number of times your heart could beat in a minute.

When you exercise, you will get the most benefit if your pulse rate rises to about 3/5 or 60% of its

maximum rate. Never make your pulse rise to more than 4/5 or 80% of the maximum level, as this puts too much strain on your heart.

Take your pulse just before and just after each exercise session and keep a record of how much the rate has increased.

Posture

Your posture is the way you hold yourself, whether standing, sitting or lying down. Good posture is very important for dance, as it helps you move and look better.

For good posture, your shoulders should be relaxed and level, your head up and your spine straight. Try the exercise on the right to improve your posture.

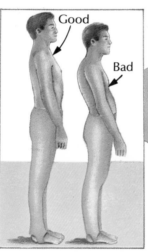

Good

Bad

Posture exercise

Starting position

Back flat

Lie on a carpet with your knees bent and pressed together. Place your hands by your thighs and keep your feet parallel and flat on the floor.

Try to make the whole of your back touch the floor. Relax your shoulders. Don't bend your neck - keep it "long" (stretched out straight).

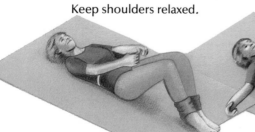

Keep shoulders relaxed.

Arms come out to sides.

Fingers touch above head then sweep down.

To improve your posture, do this exercise regularly, repeating it four times.

Breathe in deeply. At the same time, form your arms into an oval in front of you, with your fingers touching below your waist. Keep the rest of your body still.

Breathe out slowly, pushing your stomach towards the floor and sweeping each arm out sideways in a wide arc. Try to keep your back flat.

Still breathing out, continue moving your arms up to form an oval above your head. Then sweep them down in an arc to the starting position.

53

Warm-up exercises

Here are some warm-up exercises to try. Repeat each of them three or four times.

Take care not to overdo it though. If any muscles feel painful afterwards, soaking in a warm bath should ease them. If the muscles are very painful for several days, see your doctor.

Checklist for warming up

1 Wear loose, comfortable clothes.

2 Exercise in a warm place where there is plenty of space.

3 Exercise on a carpeted or sprung wood floor.

4 Before you start check your posture and practise breathing properly (see pages 52-53).

Remember, while doing these exercises, try to keep your stomach pulled in, your back straight and your bottom tucked in.
Don't worry if you can't manage all this at first. Keep trying, and have fun.

The centre of movement

Your centre of movement is the dance term for the mid-point of your body where all dance moves begin.

Knowing where your centre of movement is helps you keep your balance when you are dancing. If you pull in your stomach and imagine that it is touching your spine, the point where it touches is your centre.

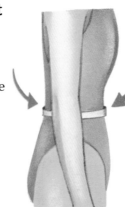

Warming up your feet

Your feet bear all your weight, so they need to be supple, especially when you are dancing. To warm them up, find a smooth pole or broom handle. Sit up straight on a hard chair. Place the pole on the floor in front of you and put one foot on it. Roll the foot forwards and backwards, keeping it on the pole. Then do the same with the other foot.

Head roll

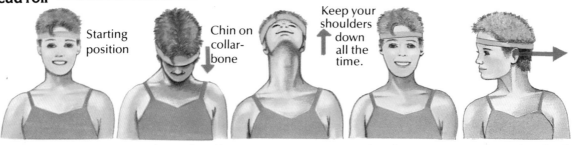

Starting position · Chin on collar-bone · Keep your shoulders down all the time.

Stand with feet slightly apart, back straight and shoulders down. Look straight ahead.

Tilt your head forwards. Then tilt it back slowly, opening your mouth. Then close your mouth.

Centre your head again, then tilt it forwards. Then return to centre again smoothly.

Turn your head to the right and return to centre. Then turn it to the left and return to centre.

Shoulder shrugs

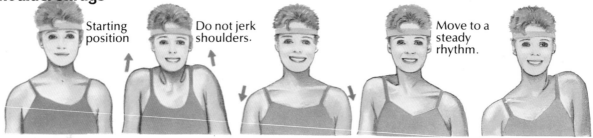

Starting position · Do not jerk shoulders. · Move to a steady rhythm.

Stand in the starting position (see head roll), arms hanging loosely by your sides.

Lift both shoulders towards your ears, then push them down. Repeat four times.

Now raise your shoulders alternately so that when one is up the other is down, like a seesaw.

Return to the starting position after each movement. Repeat four times.

Arm swings

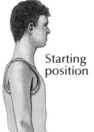  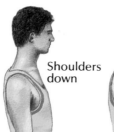 

Starting position

Keep body still.

Shoulders down

Start in the usual position, but with your feet slightly further apart for balance.

Swing your arms up in front of you to shoulder height. Then return them to your sides.

Next, swing them out sideways to shoulder height. Then return them to your sides.

Now revolve your arms in two big backward circles. Try to keep the rest of your body still.

Waist bend

  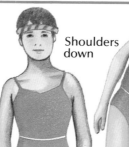 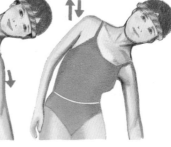

Shoulders down

Stand in the starting position, with feet quite wide apart, arms relaxed.

Bend sideways to the right, sliding your right arm down your right leg.*

Return to centre. Bend to the left, with your left arm sliding down your left leg.

Holding the bent position, bounce up and down from the waist four times.

Waist twist

 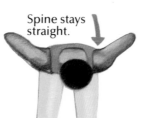 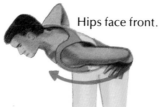 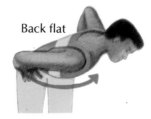

Spine stays straight.

Hips face front.

Back flat

Stand in the starting position, but with your hands on your hips. Bend forwards from the waist.

Keep your upper body parallel with the floor and your back flat. Don't bend your neck.

Slowly revolve your upper body, or torso, to the right from the waist. Keep your hips still.

Revolve your torso to the left in the same way. Repeat to each side four times.

Leg stretches

  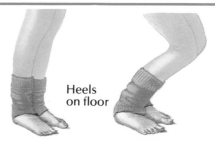 

Keep your body still.

Heels on floor

Stand in the starting position but with your hands on your hips and your feet together.

Rise up on the balls of your feet. Then bring your heels back down so you return to the start.

Immediately bend your knees as far as you can, while keeping your heels flat on the floor.

You should feel your calf muscles stretch as your knees bend. Now straighten up again.

*When you repeat this exercise, start by bending to the left.

Learning to dance

If you want to learn contemporary, jazz or tap dance, you will need to take classes. To make good progress you must attend regularly. One class a week is enough for a beginner, but if you want to be a really good dancer you will have to build up to three classes a week or more. You can find out more about taking dance classes on these two pages.

Most people pick up popular dances such as rock 'n' roll or breakdancing at discos and parties. It is possible to take classes in these styles, but you may have to hunt around to find them.

Choosing a dance class

Before paying for a course of classes, ask if you can watch one first. This will help you decide whether you like this type of dance, and whether you enjoy the teacher's approach. If possible, take a friend who has some dancing experience when you first go to watch a class.

Some dance studios let you take one or two trial classes before registering for a full course.

Check that the teacher has proper qualifications. He or she should be trained as a professional dance teacher, or should have danced with a good professional dance company.

Training your body

Learning to dance well is hard work. There may be times when your muscles hurt and you feel that you are not getting anywhere. But don't be discouraged. Even professional dancers have to face up to disappointments sometimes.

Don't overdo your training, especially at first. You are more likely to lose heart if you tire yourself out. When you practise at home, be careful: it is best just to do simple warm-up exercises (see pages 54-55) or moves which you have learnt in class.

Follow the tips on pages 52-53 about looking after your muscles. Remember, although dancing is a discipline, it should also be fun.

At a dance class

Each dance teacher has his or her own teaching style, but most dance classes are divided into stages. In some kinds of dance, for example contemporary, the classes follow quite a strict pattern. For other styles classes are less formal.

It is a good idea to get to the class early so you can do your own warm-up exercises before it starts.

During the class your teacher will probably move round the studio to see how each student is getting on. Don't be afraid to ask the teacher to show you how to do a movement again if you are not sure about it.

A contemporary class

One of the most common contemporary dance techniques is Graham technique (see pages 60-61), named after Martha Graham.

A Graham class is divided into three stages. The class starts with "floorwork". This involves doing simple exercises either sitting or lying on the floor. These help to increase the suppleness of your spine and limbs.

The second stage of a Graham class is called centrework. You do exercises standing up, but staying in one place. These help you develop better balance and a sense of your centre of movement.

The third stage of a Graham class involves moving in space. This means doing travelling steps, and sequences which help your co-ordination.

A jazz class

In a jazz class you start with warm-up exercises. You then do exercises to improve your sense of rhythm, which is very important for jazz dance. Part of the class also involves learning isolations. An isolation is the movement of one part of your body separately from the rest of it. Isolations are a vital part of jazz dance.

In the last part of the class you usually do a sequence of movements which has been worked out, or choreographed, by the teacher. The sequence is built up gradually, starting off with simple steps. As your dancing improves, the sequence gets more complicated and different movements are added.

A tap class

The first part of a tap class concentrates on warming up your feet by bouncing up and down and jumping.

You then do basic steps, such as forward and backward taps, to fairly slow rhythms. This allows you to practise doing the steps using the correct part of the foot.

Then you work to a faster rhythm and combine the basic moves to make patterns of fast steps called time steps. You learn various routines, which you repeat and add to at each class. You may also spend part of the class learning to dance in time to music and with a partner.

A rock 'n' roll class

In the first class you learn how to hold your partner and how to move your feet in time to the music.

You warm up and get used to working with a partner by doing exercises like holding both hands and bouncing on the spot together. This helps the two of you to co-ordinate your movements, ready for doing more difficult routines.

Then you start learning rock 'n' roll moves, such as twirls and spins. Rock 'n' roll dancing is made up of sequences of these moves fitted into the rhythm of the steps you are doing with your feet. As you progress the moves become more complex and energetic.

In each class you practise the basic moves and learn some new ones.

Contemporary dance

Contemporary dance began at the end of the 19th century. A number of people felt that classical ballet put too many restrictions on how the body could move and limited the way dancers could express their feelings.

Two American dancers, Isadora Duncan and Loie Fuller, became pioneers of modern dance. Isadora Duncan developed a very free dance style, making sweeping movements with her body. Loie Fuller used dramatic lighting and costumes to create fantasy effects.

Opposite you can find out about some other pioneers of contemporary dance.

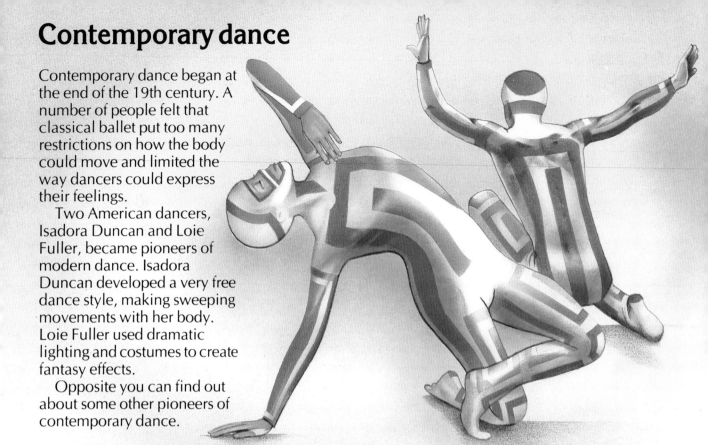

The aims of contemporary dance

Contemporary dance is concerned with expressing your own feelings, so it is a very flexible kind of dance. Because feelings and thoughts vary from person to person, contemporary dancers continually explore and discover new ways of moving. They do not have to keep to a fixed technique.

Men and women have equal importance on the contemporary dance stage. They do not have to fit into traditional roles as they usually do in classical ballet. Below you can see some differences between classical ballet and contemporary dance.

Ballet	Contemporary dance
1 The shapes and patterns the dancers make nearly always look graceful and beautiful.	1 Dance can show the ugly as well as the beautiful things that exist in life.
2 The body must be a particular size and shape and is trained from a young age to achieve this.	2 The body can be any weight and height provided it is strong and supple.
3 Dancers look light and leap through the air as if they are defying gravity.	3 Many movements are based on the floor. Dancers use the pull of gravity to tilt and fall.
4 The basic steps are strictly defined. Every dancer learns these movements.	4 There are many different styles of dancing which require various sorts of training.
5 Dances usually follow a story line and include different characters.	5 Dances are often about ideas or moods, instead of telling a definite story.
6 Dancers wear special clothes, such as tutus, which show their movements clearly. Women wear special shoes for dancing on *pointes* (tiptoe).	6 Dancers wear all sorts of different clothes. They may wear very casual or very elaborate costumes. They often dance barefoot.

The Denishawn School

In 1914 two American dancers called Ruth St. Denis and Ted Shawn founded a dance school called the Denishawn School. Their dancing was modern and very theatrical. The school taught dance styles from all over the world, for instance Japanese dance. It encouraged dancers to invent new techniques.

Many students from Denishawn went on to become pioneers of contemporary dance.

Martha Graham

Martha Graham was a student at the Denishawn School. She developed her own contemporary dance technique and in 1927 founded the Martha Graham school in New York.

She also became famous for her dramatic dance performances (see page 84). Her style contrasted very closed-in positions with free and open ones. Many contemporary dance schools now teach a technique based on hers.

Rudolf von Laban

Rudolf von Laban's ideas influenced modern dance styles in the 1920s. Laban was a teacher and creator of dances working in Germany. He analyzed movement in a scientific way to show how it could express things more clearly.

His geometric sketches showed how different gestures like reaching out or crouching down could change the way the body fitted into a space.

Merce Cunningham

Merce Cunningham is an American dancer whose work has had a big impact on contemporary dance. After working with Martha Graham, he founded his own dance group in 1953. It is now one of the most famous contemporary dance companies in the world.

Cunningham's style combines elegance with natural movements to create a flowing and relaxed effect.

Post-modern dance

Post-modern dance first emerged in New York in the 1960s. The term refers to the various experimental forms of contemporary dance which have developed since then.

Some post-modern ideas about dance include the use of improvisation (when dancers make up the movements on the spot), speech, video and film in dances. Post-modern dances have been performed in unusual places, such as art galleries.

New styles of dance are always being developed as contemporary dancers experiment with different ways of moving.

Graham-based exercises

These pages show some contemporary dance exercises for you to try. They are based on Martha Graham's technique and are divided into floorwork, centrework, and moving in space (see page 57).

As you do each movement, try to concentrate on how it feels. Picture to yourself what you are trying to do, as shown on the right. Repeat each exercise several times using both sides of your body.

To help you keep your back and neck straight, imagine you are being pulled up by a string tied to the top of your head.

Floorwork

Floorwork exercises are done sitting, kneeling or lying down. They help you control your body better and make your spine supple. Since you stay in one place and move slowly, floorwork exercises help you to concentrate on your body and how each movement feels.

Try to use the floor as a working surface: don't just lean on it, but push down against it to give more strength to your movements.

Sitting spine stretch

Relax head and neck.

You may not be able to bend this far at first.

Sit with your knees bent and the soles of your feet pressed together. Rest your hands on your ankles and keep your back straight.

Bend forwards slowly as far as you can, breathing out. Keep your bottom on the floor and your legs still. Then straighten up slowly.

Parallel leg flexes

Keep left leg straight.

Keep back straight.

Sit with your legs and arms parallel and straight out in front. Point your feet.

Bend your right knee, flexing, or bending, the right foot towards you. Return to the start.

Do the same exercise but flex the left foot and point the right foot. Keep your back straight.

Now flex and point each leg in turn, without stopping in between each movement.

Contractions

The movement called a contraction is central to Graham technique. It gets its name from the contracting, or tightening, of the stomach muscles. This frees the pelvis and stretches the spine so they are ready for movement.

In its simplest form the contraction is a fairly small movement. You should be able to feel the movement even though it may not show very much. Try to imagine that you are lengthening your spine, not squashing it.

Clasp your hands in front.

Keep shoulders still . . .

. . . and directly over hips.

Sit cross-legged with arms out in front at shoulder height. To the count of three, tighten your buttock muscles, pull your stomach in, and push your pelvis forward.

Hold the contraction for a moment. Slowly return to the start. This is called releasing. Your body should not sag or slump as you do it. Repeat the exercise three times.

Centrework

Centrework exercises are done standing in one place. They aim to build strength in your limbs and back and to develop your sense of your centre of movement (see page 54).

You do centrework exercises both with your legs parallel and with your legs in a turned-out position, knees and toes facing out to the sides.

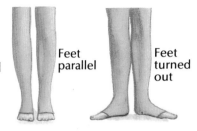

Feet parallel

Feet turned out

Parallel *demi-pliés*

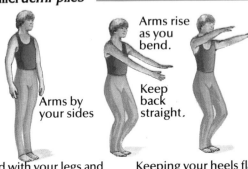

Arms by your sides

Arms rise as you bend.

Keep back straight.

Imagine you are pushing against the air.

Full *plié*

Arms straight up

Heels off floor

Stand with your legs and feet parallel, about 10 cm (4 in) apart.

Keeping your heels flat on the floor, bend your knees as far as you can.

Come back up, bending then pushing out your arms. Return to start.

Repeat three times. In class you will also do a full *plié* (shown above).

Leg beats

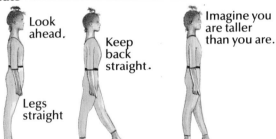
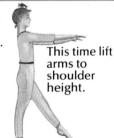
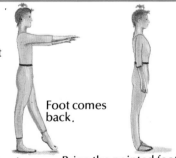

Look ahead.

Keep back straight.

Imagine you are taller than you are.

Legs straight

This time lift arms to shoulder height.

Foot comes back.

Stand with feet parallel. Slide your left foot out until it is pointed.

Then close it back to the starting position.

Now slide the foot out until it leaves the floor.

Bring the pointed foot back to the floor and slide it back to the start.

Moving in space

The exercise below is a walk to a three-beat rhythm, involving one long, low step and two short, high ones. As you do the exercise, imagine that your body topples forward but is caught just in time by the leg you are stepping on to. To help you balance, imagine the movement starts from deep inside.

Triplet

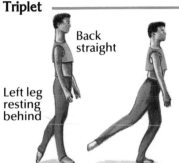

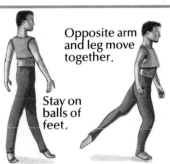
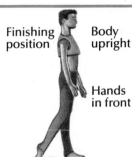

Back straight

Left leg resting behind

Opposite arm and leg move together.

Legs straight

Stay on balls of feet.

Finishing position

Body upright

Hands in front

Stand with your weight on your right leg. Take a long step forward on to your left leg. Bring your right arm forward.

Still moving forward, take a short step with your right leg, rising up on the balls of your feet. Move your left arm forward.

Then take a short step with your left leg.
Go straight into the next triplet taking a long step with your right leg.

Keep doing triplets until you are moving rhythmically. Finish neatly, with your weight on one leg.

61

Cunningham-based exercises

The exercises on these two pages are based on Merce Cunningham's approach to movement.

Cunningham does not write down his exercises in a final form. This means that he is the only person who teaches pure Cunningham technique, but these exercises will give you an idea of his dance method.

Cunningham's style emphasizes the upright position and these exercises are all done standing up. They aim to develop the suppleness of your spine and the strength of your legs. Try to move gracefully, with your arms and legs making neat, clear lines, so the movements look elegant.

Demi-pliés

All the exercises on these two pages involve doing a *demi-plié*, or knee-bend. This movement can be done with the feet turned out or parallel.

To do a *demi-plié*, bend your knees as far as you can, keeping your heels flat. Try to keep your knees directly above your middle toes. Keep your head up – this helps your balance. Imagine that you stay the same height, even though your knees are bent.

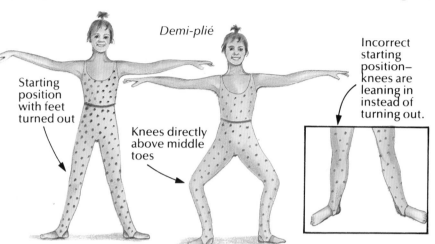

Demi-plié

Starting position with feet turned out

Knees directly above middle toes

Incorrect starting position– knees are leaning in instead of turning out.

Exercise 1

Hands turned inwards

Legs straight

Drop head and arms forward.

Arms at shoulder height

Demi-plié

Heels stay on floor.

Stand with your feet turned out and slightly apart. Hold your arms out to the sides at shoulder height.

Keeping your legs straight, curve your back out, so your upper body, or torso, drops forward to waist level.

Flatten your back until it is parallel with the floor. Open your arms out again and do a *demi-plié* (see above).

Keeping your back flat, straighten your legs. Bring your torso upright smoothly so you are back at the start.

Exercise 2

Torso turned to right

Curve back.

Torso facing front

Bring torso back up.

Hips facing front

Balance weight in centre.

Demi-plié

Legs straight

Stand with feet parallel and slightly apart. Hold your arms out to the sides at shoulder height. Look straight ahead.

Do a *demi-plié* and twist your torso to the right. Keep your hips facing the front and your heels on the floor.

Keeping your torso turned to the right, curve your back out. Then swivel your torso to face the front again.

Flatten your spine and straighten your legs out of the *demi-plié*. Then bring your torso upright again smoothly.

Exercise 3

Keep arms in same position.

Stand with your feet parallel, and your right arm held up. Bend forwards from the waist, curving your spine.

Hips face front.

Return to the start. Then curve your torso to the right. Keep your arms in the same position all the time.

Keep legs straight.

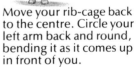
Left arm comes up.

Then, in one movement, shift your rib-cage to the left, lowering your right arm. Bring your left arm out to the side.

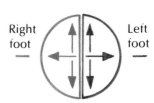
Move your rib-cage back to the centre. Circle your left arm back and round, bending it as it comes up in front of you.

Arm bent

Demi-plié

Continue moving your arm up and do a _demi-plié_, tilting your head back so you are looking at the ceiling.

Arm finishes above your head.

Straighten your spine and legs. You are now in the starting position. Repeat the sequence on the left side.

Exercise 4

In this exercise you point your foot forward, to the side, to the back and to the side again. You make a semi-circle with your foot.

Then you do the same thing with the opposite foot, so that the whole exercise makes a complete circle (see right).

The first row of pictures below shows you how to do the sequence pointing your foot to the front.

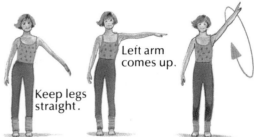
Right foot   Left foot

Work to a steady count, one beat for each movement.

Look straight ahead.

Stand with your feet turned out, your heels together and your arms out to the sides.

Slide your right foot out in front and point it. Pull up on the muscles of your left leg to help your balance.

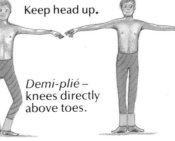
Keep head up.

Demi-plié – knees directly above toes.

Bring your right foot back to the start and bend your knees in a _demi-plié_. Then straighten your knees.

Keep back straight.

Point the foot out again, and close back, but this time keep your legs straight as you close back.

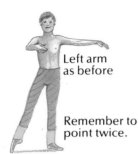
Left arm as before

Remember to point twice.

Now repeat the sequence, but pointing your right foot out to the side, with your right arm curved out in front.

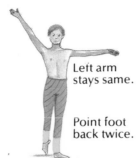
Left arm stays same.

Point foot back twice.

Repeat the sequence pointing your right foot out behind. Hold your right arm up in a diagonal line.

Finally repeat the sequence pointing the right foot out to the side again. Hold the right arm curved out in front.

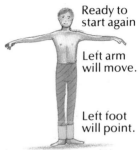
Ready to start again

Left arm will move.

Left foot will point.

Do the whole exercise as before, but pointing the left foot and moving the left arm instead of the right.

Jazz dance

Jazz dance is energetic and expressive. It is great fun to do and improves your co-ordination. Nowadays, most of the dance you see in musicals, films and pop videos is jazz dance.

You can be any shape or size to do jazz dance. It is best to start learning when you are about 13 and your bone structure has grown quite strong. This is because jazz movements put a lot of stress on the spine and pelvis. Make sure you go to a fully qualified teacher.

Jazz dance has some very distinct characteristics. You can find out about four of these below.

Rhythm

Rhythm and co-ordination are the most important aspects of jazz dance. You need to be able to express the rhythm of the music in your movements. When you start jazz classes you usually dance to pop music which has a strong, simple beat. True jazz music has more complicated rhythms.

Syncopation

Listen to a piece of music and clap in time to it. Now listen again but this time clap in between the beats. You are syncopating the rhythm. This is an important skill in jazz dance. As you practise syncopating you will learn to hear all the possible rhythms of the music you dance to.

Hip swinging

Jazz dance includes many hip and pelvic movements, which are used to reflect rhythms and make expressive poses. Swinging your hips also helps to develop the quick reaction to rhythms which is essential in jazz dance.

Isolation

An isolation is moving one part of the body while keeping the rest of it still or moving in a different direction. Like hip swinging, this emphasizes the rhythms of the music by repeating them with the body. It looks as if the music is played right through you.

Isolation has become a very sophisticated skill which is also used by body poppers (see page 78).

Different types of jazz

Jazz dance is always changing, partly because it allows dancers to make up their own steps and because it is danced to various kinds of music.

There are several distinct styles. One of the most popular is Rock or Funk Jazz which is danced to pop music. It is a powerful, dynamic style which is taught in many jazz classes today.

There are three, more specialized styles called Traditional, Gospel and Afro-Caribbean Primitive. These are quite similar to the earliest forms of jazz dance created by Africans (see opposite).

Broadway Jazz is a more polished, flamboyant style. It developed when jazz dance became a form of professional entertainment in the 1920s. It is named after Broadway, a street in New York where there are lots of theatres and dance shows. Broadway is a glamorous, punchy kind of jazz which is exciting to watch.

Learning jazz

Many jazz classes are available in studios, schools and dance colleges. Although jazz dance can be very free and creative, when you start you have to concentrate on learning the technique and basic steps.

Like other kinds of dancing, jazz is a discipline in which you need to control your body. You learn to move with and interpret the music.

The main thing is not to get impatient or discouraged. Be prepared to feel quite hopeless and silly in class for a few weeks. If you persevere you will have lots of fun. With practice you will be able to make up your own jazz dances and as your technique improves, you can try more specialized styles.

Jazz music

Jazz music developed with jazz dance as part of the new black culture in America from the 17th century onwards. The main jazz instruments are saxophone, piano, double bass, trumpet and drums. The music has varied rhythms and great energy which make you feel like dancing. For many years jazz dance was performed only to jazz music, but since the 1940s it has been danced to other types of popular music with good rhythms.

At the back of this book there is a list of records which have exciting rhythms to dance to. Listen to a few and see which ones make you want to get up and dance.

The African roots of jazz

Jazz dance developed from African tribal dances. These were brought to the Caribbean and to America by African slaves in the 17th and 18th centuries. Over the years the slaves' dances were influenced by dances from the cultures in which they were forced to live.

During the 19th century, entertainments known as minstrel shows developed, involving singing and dancing to jazz music. At first they were performed only by black dancers for black audiences.

Then in the 1920s jazz music and dancing became hugely popular with both blacks and whites and spread to Europe. The minstrel shows were taken over by professional dancers who brought new skills and training to the jazz style.

At the same time movements from European dances such as the Foxtrot were gradually blended into the jazz style.

As popular music changed in the 1940s and '50s so did the dancing and it was during this period that modern jazz styles evolved.

Jazz exercises

On these two pages there are some jazz exercises to try. Each teacher interprets jazz techniques in an individual way, so you may learn different exercises at your class.

It is best to do the exercises in the order in which they appear here, because this will help your body get used to the sort of movements involved.

The stretch exercises improve suppleness by stretching out your muscles.

Then the isolation exercise teaches you how to move one part of your body separately from the rest of it. You can then go on to do more dramatic moves, such as the jazz turn and walk.

Stretch Exercise 1

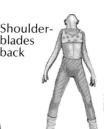

Arms loosely by your sides

Shoulder-blades back

Knees stay bent.

Hands touch floor.

Arms relaxed

Stand with your feet wide apart and parallel. Then bend your knees and push your bottom out. Drop your head back.

Bend forward from the waist and hollow the lower part of your spine. Keep your shoulder-blades back but relaxed.

Lean right down from the waist, letting your back curve outwards. Drop your head and arms forward.

Straighten your knees and spine, gradually bringing your torso upright so that you are back in the starting position.

Stretch Exercise 2

Shoulders down and relaxed

Torso faces front.

Don't tilt head up.

Relax arms.

You can bend your knees slightly to help you.

Stand with your feet turned out, wide apart and your arms straight up. Stretch to the right.

Keeping your back straight, bend from the waist so that your torso is parallel with the floor.

Pull your leg muscles up, and reach down over your right leg so your hands touch the floor.

Swing your torso across to the centre, so your head and arms are dropped loosely between your feet.

Hip directly over leg

Back flat

Legs straight

Swing your torso through to the left side, so you are reaching over your left leg. Make sure your back is flat.

Swing your torso up so it is parallel to the floor, pointing to the left. Straighten your arms.

Then bring your torso up to the left, so you are looking to the front while stretching to the left.

Bring your torso upright to return to the start. Repeat the sequence, this time stretching to the left first.

Pelvic isolation

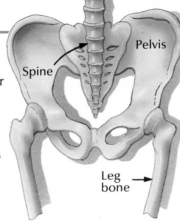

The pelvis is the circle of bone formed by your hips. It joins your leg bones to the base of your spine.

The pelvis is used a lot in jazz dance. It acts like a lever pushing your back or legs into action. It also links movements in your torso with movements in your legs, to make a flowing sequence which runs through your whole body.

To use your pelvis in these ways you need to be able to move it separately from the rest of your body. The exercise on the right and below shows you how to do this.

Spine

Pelvis

Leg bone

Starting position (front view)

Hands splayed out

Stand with your feet slightly apart and parallel, your knees bent and your elbows tucked in.

  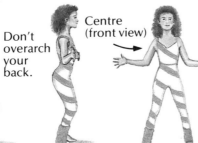  

Starting position (side view)

Don't overarch your back.

Centre (front view)

Make moves small and precise.

Tilt your pelvis forward. Bring it back to the centre. Try to keep the rest of the body still.

Tilt your pelvis back slightly, so your bottom juts out. Return to the centre.

Push your pelvis to the right, so your right hip nearly touches your elbow. Return to centre.

Push your pelvis left and return to centre. Now repeat the whole sequence four times.

Jazz step turn

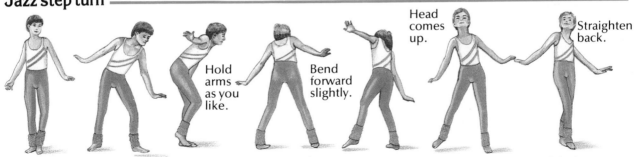

Hold arms as you like.

Bend forward slightly.

Head comes up.

Straighten back.

In this exercise you do a complete turn. Start with your feet together. Step out on to your left foot.

As you step on to your left leg, pivot on your left foot and then step on to your right leg.

Pivot on your right foot, bring your left foot round to the left. Finish with your weight on your left foot.

Bring your right foot to join your left, so you are back at the start. Now go back the other way.

Jazz walk

Lift right heel off floor.

Straighten left leg.

Move arms as you like.

Stand letting your weight sag to your right. Step to the left, pushing your weight to the right.

Bring your right leg to join your left. As your right foot moves across swing your weight to the left.

While your feet are together, shift your weight back to the right. Now step out again to the left.

Repeat the movements in a smooth sequence, so you travel sideways. Then go the other way.

Tap dance

Tap dancing is one of the most stylish kinds of dance and a fun way to exercise. It is a dance where you create your own sound with your feet so you do not need to rely on music. The main qualities you need are a good sense of rhythm and timing, and a love of performing to an audience.

The essential movements of tap come from your feet and ankles. Your arms, head and hands are important, but they move to complement the actions of your feet.

Tap styles

Tap is an American dance, but it has also developed in England with a slightly different style. The main feature of American tap, known as jazz tap, is the looseness of the body which makes the style look very fluid and elegant.

In England a European style of tap has developed which is more closely related to Irish and English clog dances. It is a bouncy style with the body held more rigidly.

Whatever the style, the important thing about tap is that dancers improvise and express themselves.

How tap started

Tap dance started in America in the 19th century. Its roots are in the Irish jig and English clog dances of early settlers, mingled with the African tribal dances brought by slaves. The European jigs involved intricate leg and footwork, while the Africans danced flat-footed, moving their whole body to the pounding rhythms of their drums.

Tap emerged when black slaves on the American plantations combined their rhythms with the jigs and clog dances. White people began to copy the black dancers and tap eventually became a performance dance. People started to wear special tap shoes with metal plates on the soles and to learn a basic technique.

Tap dancing reached the height of its popularity in the 1930s through Hollywood film musicals. These starred tap artists such as Fred Astaire, Bill Robinson, Eleanor Powell and Gene Kelly. Fred Astaire was probably the most famous. He was trained in ballet and his tap style was distinctively graceful and elegant.

Tap shoes

You can buy special shoes with toe and heel taps or have taps fitted to ordinary shoes. The shoes should be soft and flexible, should cover your whole foot and have a slight heel. (Stilettos or sling-backs are no good.)

Before you buy any shoes make sure they fit you very well and that you can bend your toes up when you are wearing them.

The best clothes to wear for tap are a leotard and tights or loose-fitting trousers and a top.

Music for tap

Tap dance was first performed to jazz music and is best suited to the irregular rhythms of jazz. Jazz music changed over the years and so tap was done to Charleston music in the 1920s, swing music in the '30s and be-bop in the '40s.

Today people tend to tap-dance to music from old films such as *Singing in the Rain* and *Tea for Two*.

Preparing to tap

Your feet do most of the work in tap dance and it is important they are warmed up before you begin.

Here are some warm-up exercises to try. For the first two sit on a chair or hold on to a support.

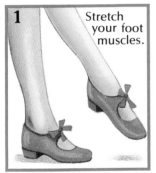

1 Stretch your foot muscles.

Start with your feet parallel on the floor. Lift your left foot off the ground and then point it down as far as you can.

Then bring your foot up as far as you can, flexing your toes. Repeat the down and up movement slowly, four times.

Do the same with your right foot. This exercise helps to strengthen your ankle, so you can tap with a clear, crisp sound.

4

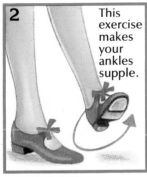

2 This exercise makes your ankles supple.

Raise your left leg and point your foot straight up. Circle your foot round slowly. Repeat the exercise four times.

Then circle your foot four times in the opposite direction. Repeat the whole exercise with your right foot.

3 Bounce eight times.

Stand on the balls of your feet and bounce up and down without leaving the ground or allowing your heels to touch the ground.

Try this exercise to practise using the ball of your foot separately from the heel. Walk to a steady rhythm lifting your legs a few inches off the floor in a strutting movement. With each step bring the ball of your foot down on to the floor first, then the heel.

As you take each step swing the arm opposite to the leg which is lifted.

Tap steps

To tap-dance you relax your body and strike the ground smartly with the ball or heel of your foot. The tap should make one clear ringing sound.

On these two pages there are some basic tap steps for you to try. Practise each one with both feet. When you have mastered the basic steps there are suggestions for putting several together to make a tap sequence.

Before you start

1. Make sure that you are practising on a good tap surface such as wood or hard linoleum. You can buy a special tap mat or make one out of a piece of plywood.

2. When you are tapping, count to a steady rhythm "1 and 2 and 3 and 4 and". Most of the time you tap on the number, but sometimes you tap on the "and" as well so you are tapping twice as quickly as usual.

3. Keep your knees and ankles as loose and flexible as you can and try to produce a clear, crisp sound when you tap.

Straight tap

Stand on your right foot. Extend your left leg so your foot is just off the ground.

Now strike the ground sharply with the ball of your left foot. Keep your knee still.

Finish the tap with your left foot pointing up and held off the ground. Keep your right foot still.

Forward tap

Stand on your left foot, with your right foot lifted up behind. Relax your knees.

Move your foot and leg forwards from the knee tapping the ground once as you go.

Finish with your right foot pointing upwards and held off the ground. Keep your left foot still.

Backward tap

Stand on your left foot and extend your right leg in front, pointing your right foot up.

Move your right foot backwards, tapping the ground once as your foot comes back.

Finish with your right foot just off the ground, toes pointing down towards the floor.

Shuffle

A shuffle combines the movement of a forward and backward tap as shown in these pictures. It is done very quickly. Count a steady beat "1 and 2" and try to do the shuffle so you tap forward on "and", then backward on 2.

Hop

Stand on the ball of your left foot with your knee slightly bent and your right foot off the ground. Now hop, lifting your left foot clear of the floor and landing on the ball of your foot so that you make a single sound. Try not to wobble as you land.

Shuffle hop

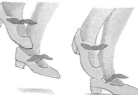

This combination of a shuffle and a hop makes three tap sounds. Try it slowly at first. Tap forward with your right foot on 1, back on 2, hop on your left foot on 3 and hold the position for 4. Then speed it up: tap forward on 1, back on "and", hop on 2, hold for "and". Repeat on "3 and 4 and".

Arm positions

You can use lots of different arm positions when you are tapping. Here are three to try. Decide which looks and feels best by practising them in front of a mirror.

Parallel

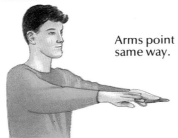

Arms point same way.

In this position both arms reach out in the same direction, without touching.

Co-ordinated

Arms at different angles.

Your arms are stretched out in the same direction, but at different angles to one another.

In opposition

Arms point opposite ways.

In this position your arms reach in opposite directions, one forward, the other back or out to the side.

Tap sequences

The following sequences are combinations of the steps shown on these two pages. As you do the steps, count steadily to eight as shown. The counts which are underlined are where the tap sounds occur. R stands for right foot and L for left. It is a good idea to do the sequences to music, so that you get used to dancing to a rhythm.

Sequence 1	
One	Forward tap R
and two	Backward tap R
and three	Forward tap R
and four	Backward tap R
and five	Shuffle R
and six	Shuffle R
and seven	Shuffle R
and eight	Step on to R
Repeat using your left foot.	

Sequence 2	
One	Forward tap L
and two	Backward tap L
and three	Hop R
and four	Step sideways on to L
and five	Forward tap R
and six	Backward tap R
and seven	Hop L
and eight	Step sideways on to R

More tap steps

Here are the names of some more tap steps which you may learn at your classes.

Step A single tap sound made by stepping on to the ball of the foot.

Tap, step Two tap sounds made by doing a forward or backward tap followed immediately by a step.

Heel beat* A single tap sound made by raising the heel keeping the ball on the floor, then replacing the heel.

Tip of the toe beat A single tap sound made by raising the foot and touching the front edge of the toe tap to the floor.

Brush This is similar to a forward or backward tap but the movement is exaggerated by swinging the leg from the hip joint.

*The difference between a tap and a beat is that a tap finishes with your foot off the floor and a beat with your foot on the floor.

Rock 'n' roll

Rock 'n' roll first became well known in the 1950s when an American group, Bill Haley and the Comets, released a record called *Rock around the Clock*. American teenagers had

been dancing for some years to the heavy beat of Rhythm and Blues records that had been popular in the black community since the Second World War. New groups such as the Comets, and singers like Elvis Presley, took this music and mixed it with Country and Western to make the new sound – rock 'n' roll.

In America rock 'n' roll dancing is called the jitterbug and in Britain, jiving. Originally the jitterbug was a 1930s dance done to Big Band swing music. It was very fast and acrobatic. Now it is a slower dance, but still very exciting. You hold your partner's hand, spinning and turning.

The dance and music became a craze that spread worldwide from America.

Rock 'n' roll music

Rock 'n' roll music was fresh and lively. Most importantly, it had a simple, danceable beat and was aimed at young people. Between 1953 and 1959 lots of rock 'n' roll records were made, such as *See you later Alligator* and *Don't step on my Blue Suede Shoes*.

A 1950s juke box

Rock 'n' roll culture

Rock 'n' roll shocked many people. It seemed wild and rebellious. A whole teenage culture grew up around it with people meeting in cafés and listening to juke boxes.

In the late 1950s rock 'n' roll became commercialized and stale and new dances emerged.

Dancing rock 'n' roll

In the last few years there has been a rock 'n' roll revival. Some clubs have special rock 'n' roll nights and you can learn the dance at classes. You only need learn a few moves to start with. Then you can gradually build on them by watching other people. Below and on the next pages there are some hints on dancing rock 'n' roll and a few moves to try.

Clothes

Girls often wear full skirts which swirl round, adding to the movement and energy of the dance. Flat shoes are important for safety when you are turning and jumping. In the 1950s girls tied scarves round their necks and wore short socks.

Boys also wear 1950s style dress - baggy shirts with narrow ties, narrow trousers or denim jeans and suede shoes. In Britain a special style of dress was developed by "teddy boys" who wore long jackets, skin-tight "drainpipe" trousers and pointed shoes called winklepickers.

How to hold your partner

Here are the main rock 'n' roll holds. Partners start close together, then break away so they are at arm's length with elbows slightly bent. This gives leverage for movement. The boy moves with his legs slightly bent and shoulders hunched forward in order to provide a stable pivot for his partner. The girl does freer movements.

Closed hold - like a conventional ballroom dancing hold.

Double hold - you hold both your partner's hands.

Open hold, opposition arm - the boy's left hand holds the girl's right or vice versa.

Open hold, same arm the boy's right hand holds the girl's right hand or vice versa.

How to move your feet

Rock 'n' roll music has four beats to the bar. Your feet move in slow or quick steps. A slow step takes two beats and a quick step one.

The basic sequence of steps is shown on the right. It takes six beats (1½ bars) to complete and you repeat it over and over. These instructions are for a girl. For a boy the steps are the same but you do them with the opposite legs.

Over the page you can see how it looks when both partners do the steps.

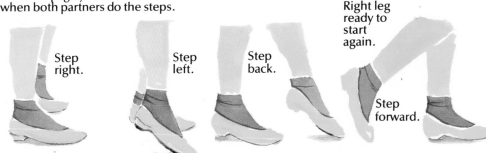

Step right.

Step left.

Step back.

Right leg ready to start again.

Step forward.

Start with your feet slightly apart. Counting 1, 2, step sideways on to your right foot, so your weight is on your right leg.

On 3, 4, step sideways on to your left foot, shifting your weight on to your left leg. (These two are slow steps.)

Then, on 5, step back on to your right foot and on 6 step forward on to your left. (These two are quick steps.)

Dancing rock 'n' roll

On these two pages you can find out how to do some rock 'n' roll moves. They are all done to a count of six. The first row of pictures below shows the steps you do with your feet (see also page 73). The other rows show moves which you do while doing these steps.

You may find it difficult to combine the footwork and moves at first. If so, don't worry about what your feet are doing, just try to get the moves right.

The basic step

Step sideways on 1,2 (left for boy, right for girl).

Step sideways on 3,4 (right for boy, left for girl).

On 5 both step back, moving away from one another.

On 6 both step forward, moving close together again.

A simple turn

Start in a closed hold. On 1, 2, both step to the side (boy to the left, girl to the right). On 3, 4, the boy steps on to his right foot and raises his left arm. The girl circles beneath, pivoting on her right foot, then stepping on to her left foot.

Arms stretched out.

Lean back slightly.

On 5, both partners step back (boy on to his left leg and girl on to her right). Pull away from one another and lean back.

On 6, both partners step forward (boy on to his right, girl on to her left) so your linked arms bend.

Slide break

Girl steps on to right foot, boy on to left.

Hold left arm out to side.

Start in a double hold. On 1, both raise your arms and turn to your left so you are facing in opposite directions.

On 2, still holding hands, bring your arms down so your left arm goes behind your head and your right arm behind your partner's.

On 3, 4, let go your hands and move apart, sliding your outstretched arm along your partner's outstretched arm.

On 5, pull away from one another, stepping back (boy on to left foot, girl on to right), then on 6 both step forward.

Spanish arms

Take small steps in order to get round the circle.

Start in a double hold. On 1, 2, the boy steps on to his left leg and raises his left arm. At the same time the girl circles a half turn to her

left so she ends up with her back to her partner and her arms crossed in front. (Girl pivots on left foot, then steps on to right.)

On 3, 4, the boy steps forward (right, left) and the girl steps back (left, right) so you move round in a circle.

On 5, 6, the boy steps back on to his right foot and raises his left arm. The girl circles right to get back to the start.

Push spin

Boy steps slightly to left of girl.

Hold right hands. On 1, 2, both step forward (boy on to his left foot, girl on to her right) and bend your arms.

On 3, the boy pushes against his partner's hand and she spins round to her right, pivoting on her right foot.

On 4, the girl completes her spin, stepping on to her left foot, and the boy catches hold of her right hand again.

On 5, 6, both partners step back (boy on to his left foot, girl on to her right) and then step forward again.

The Stroll

The Stroll is a group dance which is lots of fun to do. You stand in a line and everybody does the steps in unison. There are several different versions of the Stroll. In America the dance is done in two lines with girls facing boys.

Acrobatic rock 'n' roll

This is a mixture of rock 'n' roll and gymnastics with daring, athletic moves such as the Death Dive shown here. It was developed in Europe and is now a competition style. Couples from many countries compete in international championships.

Ceroc

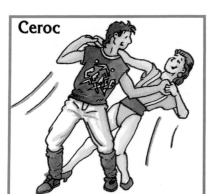

Ceroc is a new dance based on the French style of rock 'n' roll. The name comes from the French *c'est roc*. Although many ceroc moves are similar to rock 'n' roll, the dance is more upright and precise with elements of jazz and tap.

Disco dancing

The term disco dancing covers a whole range of styles, from the dancing you do with friends at a party to complex, athletic routines performed at disco dancing competitions. What all the styles have in common is that they are done to fashionable pop records.

Most people learn to disco dance by watching and copying other people. However for competition disco dancing you need to train at classes in the same way as you would for other styles.

How disco dancing started

The first discos opened in the 1960s in France (disco is short for the French word *discothèque*). At these new clubs teenagers danced to pop records, rather than to live bands as they had always done in the past. Discos quickly spread to America and Britain, encouraged by the popularity of the new "solo" dancing (dancing without holding your partner). ▶

The Twist was the first solo dance. It was a simple dance in which you pivoted on one or both feet and swivelled your hips and knees from side to side, keeping your shoulders still.

A rock 'n' roller named Chubby Checker made a record called *The Twist* and the dance became a craze. The Twist was followed by other disco dances such as the Pony, the Frug and the Madison.

Disco dancing went through a lull during the hippie period of the late 1960s. It was revived again in the '70s with another dance craze and record called the Hustle, followed by the disco-dancing film *Saturday Night Fever*.

In the '70s and '80s disco dancing has changed constantly with fashion and music. The main thing about it is that the movements are simple and repetitive so anyone can do them. There are no set rules and dances can be as simple or complicated and dramatic as the dancer wants to make them.

Disco clothes

To go to a disco you can wear almost anything that is comfortable and preferably a bit flashy. Most people wear bright, lively colours or smart white or black clothes.

For competitions, dancers wear leotards and tights, or, for boys, trousers that allow them to move freely but outline their movements clearly.

In competitions the dancers aim to outshine their rivals not just in their dancing but in their costumes, and the clothes reflect the glitter and glamour of a discothèque. Leotards and tights are made from shiny materials and are often highly decorated with coloured sequins or braid. They may have extravagant ruffles and wide, full sleeves which are tightly gathered at the cuffs.

Instead of tights, girls may wear sequinned stockings or legwarmers. They often wear glittery or beaded chokers and feathered head-dresses.

Disco dancing competitions

In 1977 following the revival of disco dancing an actor called John Travolta made the film *Saturday Night Fever* in which the hero and heroine win a disco dancing competition. The film made disco dancing hugely popular and the idea of disco dancing competitions spread to lots of different countries.

Competition disco dancing is quite different from most ordinary disco dancing. It is athletic and skilful with complex steps and routines. Dancers need to be fit and disciplined.

Competitions are organized into various age groups – under 12 years, under 16 years and adults. Dancers can compete as soloists, couples, trios (three dancers together) and teams.

The dancers compete for cups and different coloured rosettes which are awarded to the best performers. The cups may be quite elaborate, often featuring a picture of a disco dancer on a miniature shield.

Inside a disco

Today's discos are glamorous places with elaborate lighting and powerful sound systems. The disc jockeys, or DJs, who choose the music are very important because they set the style and the popularity of the club through their control over the kind of music which is played.

The disco sound

Disco music usually has a strong, simple beat which is easy to dance to. Special long versions of records are made called disco mixes. They last for about 20 minutes, allowing dancers to continue uninterrupted.

The sound quality of the records has to be very good because they are played over powerful sound systems. These have two or three turntables and a mixing deck. The mixing deck is a complex piece of equipment which allows the DJ to control the sound level, link or intermingle records and create special effects such as echoes.

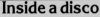

Lighting

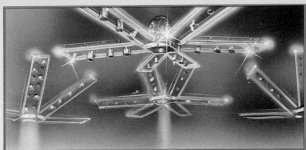

At first, disco lighting consisted of coloured light bulbs and balls with mirrors, hanging from the ceiling. As new clubs sprang up the competition for customers became fierce and lighting systems were one of the attractions.

Nowadays huge sums of money are spent on complex lighting systems, specially tailored to a disco's needs. These systems include laser beams and computerized control desks. Sometimes lighting is incorporated into or under the dance floor or into the walls to make unusual fantasy effects.

Breakdancing

Breakdancing began in the streets of New York in the 1970s and quickly became very popular. Many people learnt to do it by watching breakdancers and practising with them. You can take classes though at some dance studios.
There are two different kinds of breakdancing, called body popping and breaking.

Warning: many breakdancing moves are very dangerous. Don't try them on your own.

Body popping involves moving like a robot but more gracefully. You move each of your joints in turn very quickly. Breaking is difficult and quite dangerous. Its basic moves are floor spins and glides. Below are a body popping move and a breaking move.

Body popping – the wave

Flick left wrist up

Start with your right arm held slightly away from you. Jerk your right hand in so your elbow bends out.

Push your right hand inwards so your right shoulder is forced up until your head is resting on it. Keep your elbow bent.

Swing your head to the left and relax your right arm. Push your left shoulder up so your head rests on it and bend your left arm.

Push your left arm smoothly down and away from you. As your left shoulder comes down, push your chest out.

Breaking – the backspin

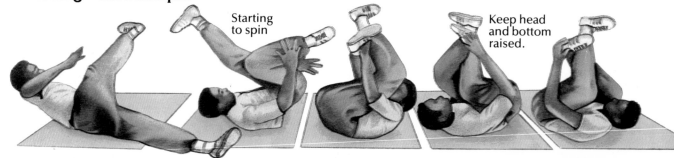

Starting to spin

Keep head and bottom raised.

Sit with your left leg stretched out, then lean on your left side. Swing your right leg up across your body, pushing your weight back.

Lift your head and bottom as your right leg swings up. Push off with your left leg and lift it off the ground. Bend your right leg in.

As you spin round, bend your left leg in. Cross your left ankle over your right so you form a tight ball. Clasp your feet with both your hands.

Tilt back slightly so you spin on your upper back, but keep your head up. Keep clasping your ankles to keep up your speed as you spin.

Breakdancing clothes

Most breakdancers wear loose-fitting, comfortable clothes that allow them to move freely. A tracksuit, or baggy trousers and a sweatshirt, are ideal. They wear tough shoes, such as trainers, tied with coloured laces to look smart.

For the more advanced moves, breakdancers need to wear knee and elbow pads, as well as a cap or hat to protect their heads when they do headspins.

Speaking the language

Breakdancing has its own special language which developed with the dancing, from words used by the street gangs in New York.

On the right there are some breakdancing words and their meanings. When you have read them, try translating what the boy is saying.

BAD · · · · good
BOX · · · · portable radio
BUCK · · · · brave
CHILLING OUT · · · · · hanging around
COOL OUT · · · relax
CREW · · · · · dance group

DEF · · · · · nice
DOGS · · · · sneakers, training shoes
FRESH · · · marvellous, fantastic
HOME BOY · · · close friend
JAM · · · · · record, song
WACK · · · · terrible, bad
ZOOTED · · · · exhausted, pooped

I was chilling out with my def box.

Uprock

Uprock was one of the first types of breakdancing to develop. It is an aggressive battle dance used by some street gangs in New York.

In an uprock session, dancers from rival gangs compete against each other. The gang members form a big circle and the dancers stand in the centre. There they perform the most difficult and dangerous moves they can and the crowd decides who is the winner.

Many of the moves of uprock are borrowed from karate and other martial arts, but in uprock the dancers do not touch each other.

Breakdancing tips

Breakdancing is most fun if you do it with friends. For example, once you have learnt to do the wave (see opposite page), you can try passing the movement on to a friend who picks up the wave where you left off.

Another thing to remember is that breakdancing should be very expressive. Many breakdancing moves originally came from mime, which is a way of talking using your body. Try to make your breakdancing tell a story in movements.

Never try difficult or dangerous breaking moves without proper instruction from a teacher.

Music and dance

A famous choreographer*, Georges Balanchine, described music as "the floor the dancer walks on". Since the earliest times, dances have developed in response to music, changing as styles of music altered.

Music and dance are very closely connected through rhythm. A rhythm is a sequence of sounds and silences of different lengths. Dance is a combination of rhythm and movement, and music is a combination of rhythm and sound. We hear rhythms everywhere around us: in the chirping of the birds, the sound of the rain, or in a dripping tap. We also feel rhythms inside our bodies, in our pulse and in our breathing.

Because we are used to hearing and feeling rhythms, when we hear music with a strong beat, it is hard for us to resist the temptation to dance to it. In this way music and dance go naturally together.

Dance music

All sorts of sounds can create dance music. Today dances are performed to music played on anything from electronic synthesizers to dustbin lids.

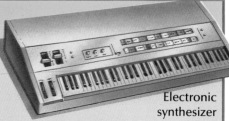

Electronic synthesizer

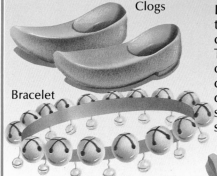

Clogs

Bracelet

In many dances the dancers themselves create the music by clapping, stamping and singing. They can make music by wearing costumes such as bracelets and clothes covered in bells, or special dance shoes, like clogs or tap shoes. They also use instruments such as tambourines.

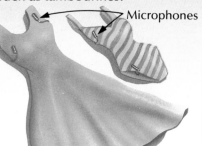

Microphones

In some post-modern dances microphones are sewn into the dancers' costumes. These amplify the dancers' breathing and the rustling of their clothes, making a kind of weird music.

Rhythm and dance

All dances are based on some kind of rhythm. When music is written down, the rhythm is shown by the different kinds of notes on the stave. These indicate the length of each sound and of the silences between the sounds, showing the exact pattern of the rhythm.

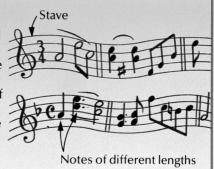

Stave

Notes of different lengths

Although a choreographer may be inspired by the emotional power of a piece of music, the dancers' movements will mainly relate to its rhythmic patterns. These provide beats for the dancers to follow and so give shape to the dance.

Most choreographers like to commission new music specially for their dances, so they can choose the rhythms on which to base the dance. Sometimes, though, they use music which has already been composed.

80 *A choreographer is someone who creates dances.

How music helps dance

Dancers moving together rely on the beat of the music to keep in time with each other and to know when they should move. This is why, when you watch a dance, the dancers can move at the same time even though they may hardly look at each other.

Music also helps to create the mood of a dance. For example, rock 'n' roll music is lively, springy, and brash. It adds to the sense of fun and energy in the dance, which is full of quick, vivid spins, leaps, and swoops.

Dance without music

Some dances have no musical accompaniment. Instead, the choreographer gives the dancers a rhythm to follow, which they carry inside them by counting silently. This provides a kind of silent "music" which goes on inside the dancers.

Merce Cunningham, a contemporary choreographer, believes that music and dance do not have to be linked. He often creates dances done in silence, or only counting out a rhythm. In performance, there may be accompanying music, but the dancers still follow the rhythms they used in rehearsal.

Making your own music

You can make all sorts of different music yourself. You can use your body to make sounds, for example, stamping your feet or clapping your hands as you move.

You can also make simple instruments to give you a wider range of sounds to dance to. Below and right there are ideas for instruments to make using household objects.

Flower-pot drum

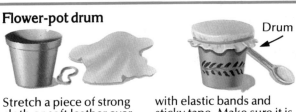

Stretch a piece of strong cloth or soft leather over the top of a flower-pot. Fasten the cloth tightly with elastic bands and sticky tape. Make sure it is taut. Use a wooden spoon as a drumstick.

Shaker

Half-fill a plastic cup with dry rice. Tape another plastic cup upside-down over the top, so the two rims are pressed together. Shake to make a light rattling sound. If you like, decorate the shaker.

Rhythm sticks

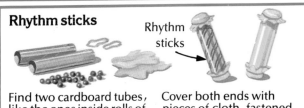

Find two cardboard tubes, like the ones inside rolls of paper towel. Fill them with pebbles or beads. Cover both ends with pieces of cloth, fastened with sticky tape or elastic bands.

Peg xylophone

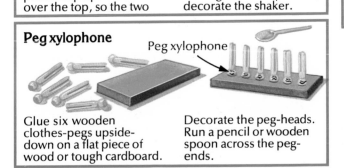

Glue six wooden clothes-pegs upside-down on a flat piece of wood or tough cardboard. Decorate the peg-heads. Run a pencil or wooden spoon across the peg-ends.

See how many soft sounds you can make, and try to match them with gentle movements. Then try making loud noises and match them with powerful, lively movements.

Put the different kinds of sound and movement together to make varied patterns. Mix them with pauses and silences. You will be creating your own music and dance.

Choreography

Choreography is the art of creating dances. The term comes from two Greek words, *khoreia* meaning choral dancing to music, and *graphia* meaning writing.

Choreography is one of the most important aspects of dance. Every time you see a dance on the stage or TV, a choreographer has decided where and how each dancer should move. To do this, a choreographer uses many different skills.

Improvisation

Two dancers improvising

Improvising means acting on the spur of the moment, without instructions and with little time to prepare what you are going to do.

Choreographers often hold improvisation sessions to find out the various ways in which dancers could perform a particular movement. Improvisation often gives choreographers new ideas.

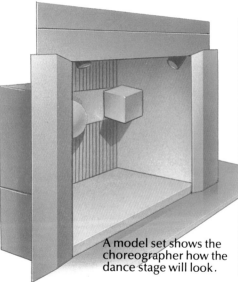

A model set shows the choreographer how the dance stage will look.

Dance notation

When a dance is choreographed, a special alphabet of signs is used to write down the movements involved in the dance.

These signs are called dance notation, or choreology. The two best-known kinds of notation are called Benesh and Labanotation.

Notation is very precise and enables a choreographer to preserve a work exactly as it was created. Learning to read and write notation is like learning a new language and takes a long time.

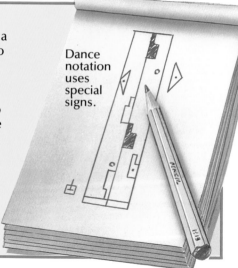

Dance notation uses special signs.

Learning to choreograph

To be a choreographer you need to know the various dance steps, why these were invented and what effects they can achieve on the stage.

Choreographers must also know how to use the stage space and must understand the basic principles of lighting and design.

Other important qualities are a good understanding of music, and plenty of imagination and original ideas. Choreographers also need to be able to work well with lots of different people and to be patient. It may take weeks to create a dance.

People often invent dances.

How choreography developed

Although people have been creating dances for thousands of years, choreography was only developed as a separate skill in the early 1900s.

As modern dance developed, traditions were overturned and the process involved in creating a dance was analyzed much more. People realized that choreography required special skills and it was recognized as an art form.

Nowadays it is possible to take courses in choreography and good choreographers are much in demand.

Creating a dance

Below you can find out about the main stages involved in creating a dance. Each choreographer has an individual way of working and the exact method used varies from dance to dance.

The first ideas

The choreographer decides on a subject for a dance. This may be inspired by anything, from a piece of music to a painting or book, or even a beautiful building.

The choreographer then chooses dancers to perform the work by holding auditions. Sometimes a dance is specially made for a particular dancer.

The choreographer and dancers explore the subject for the dance by having discussions and sometimes an improvisation session where they try out ideas.

Rehearsing the dance

The choreographer rehearses the dancers, all the time working out how the dance should develop and if it works as a whole.

As each sequence in the dance is decided, it is written down in dance notation by a professional notator, or choreologist.

The choreographer works with the lighting, set and costume designers, to produce the stage effects for the dance.

The performance

Eventually all the different elements are put together on the stage, and last-minute changes are made. The dance is now ready to be performed to an audience. This is the big moment: if anything goes wrong in the dance, the choreographer will probably get the blame!

Dance choreographers

On these two pages you can find out about some famous dance choreographers. They all began their careers as dancers, and then branched out to create brilliantly original dance styles. Even when their dances are expressing common ideas, great choreographers such as these find new ways of mixing movements together, so that dance itself never quite stands still.

Fred Astaire

Fred Astaire blended tap, ballet and ballroom dance techniques together to create a unique effect.

Astaire was born in Nebraska, America in 1900. He went to Hollywood in 1933 to appear in films. On film the subtlety and stylishness of his dancing came across very clearly. He was quickly recognized as an outstanding dancer and choreographer.

Although many of his dances were very complicated, he moved in a way that made them look effortlessly graceful.

Astaire's most famous dancing partner was Ginger Rogers. Their many films include *Top Hat* (1935) and *Swing Time* (1936).

Swing Time

Martha Graham

Lamentation

Martha Graham was born in 1894 in Pittsburgh, America. In 1916 she joined the Denishawn School of dancing but by 1923 had developed her own style.

She used strong gestures and positions that made the dancers look as if they were rooted to the earth.

Graham's dances were emotional dramas danced in a stark, ritual way. One example was her famous solo dance *Lamentation* (1930). Graham performed the whole dance sitting down, and wore a stretchy tube dress. This made her move in a way which looked restricted and painful, and which brilliantly suggested the deep misery which was the subject of the dance.

Other famous Graham dances are *Letter to the World* (1940) and *Appalachian Spring* (1944).

Alvin Ailey

Ailey is an American choreographer whose work is notable for its very intense emotional power. He uses big gestures like wide-open arm movements.

His solo for a woman dancer, *Cry*, describes the history of black women in America.

Cry

Another of his most famous dances is *Revelations*, which is danced to Negro spiritual songs.

Ailey's company, the American Dance Theater, is skilled in many techniques including ballet, Graham, jazz and African dance.

Revelations

Bob Fosse

Bob Fosse was a director, choreographer, actor and dancer. He was born in Chicago and began his career dancing in sleazy nightclubs.

Fosse choreographed dances for many films and used creative film techniques, for example, making it look as if the camera were dancing too.

His flamboyant dances were influenced by jazz technique. The most famous were in the films "Cabaret", "All That Jazz" and "Sweet Charity".

Twyla Tharp

Twyla Tharp was born in Indiana, America in 1941 and has become one of the most original contemporary dance choreographers working today. Her dance style mixes movements which suggest tap, ballet and rock influences.

Tharp's dances often look very casual and relaxed. She uses movements which seem loose, such as big sideways kicks which make the dancer look as if he or she is about to fall over. But in fact the dances rely on very complicated systems of counts. They are intricate structures, which leave nothing to chance.

Robert North

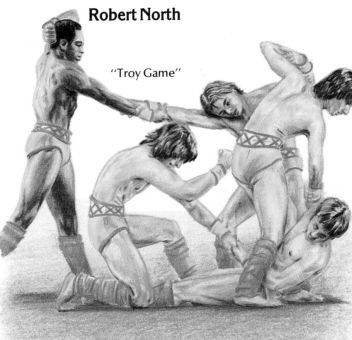

"Troy Game"

In "Push Comes To Shove", a bowler hat is passed from dancer to dancer in a slick, slapstick way.

One of Tharp's most famous works is "Raggedy Dances" (1972). It is full of attack and a sense of comedy which are typical of her work.

Robert North is an American dancer and choreographer who has worked with several major British contemporary dance companies.

His choreography is influenced by ballet technique and uses compelling music and themes which are easy to understand.

One of North's best-known works is "Troy Game", which is a funny, all-male display, involving fighting duets and athletic moves. It includes a role for a dancer who is smaller than the others and is always making mistakes. "Troy Game" is very lively and at the end the dancers fall down, apparently exhausted!

Dance companies

Most large dance companies* perform contemporary dance, for example, the London Contemporary Dance Theatre in England, the Wuppertaler Tanztheater in Germany, Paul Taylor Dance Company in America and the Australian Dance Theatre.

Groups performing other styles of dance, such as jazz and tap, tend to work in cabarets or places where they are hired for a season to perform along with comedians and other artists in a mixed show. Occasionally these groups perform in theatres.

Large and small companies

Company programmes and posters

Dance companies are much smaller than ballet companies. Even an important dance company has only about 50 staff, 15 or 20 of whom are dancers. Smaller companies have only about 15 members.

There are lots of even smaller dance groups which perform in places other than theatres. They bring dance to people who may not get the chance to see it in a theatre. They perform in schools, community or sports centres, prisons and old people's homes.

Touring

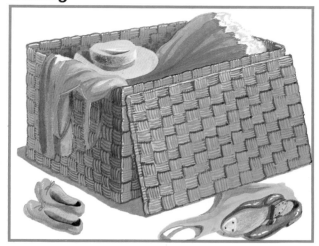

All dance companies tour, usually for about 30 weeks a year. Large companies go to each theatre for about a week. Small companies usually tour to different places every night.

Very few dance companies are based at a particular theatre.

One example is the Wuppertaler Tanztheater in Germany, which is based at the Wuppertal theatre. Other companies are based in dance centres which have rehearsal studios and staff offices but often nowhere to perform.

Jobs in a dance company

Opposite you can find out about the main jobs involved in running a dance company.

In large companies each job is done by a different person who may have several assistants. In smaller companies several jobs are done by one person and the dancers themselves take on many extra tasks.

Most dance companies are too small to pay for resident choreographers, designers and musicians. These artists are hired to work on specific pieces.

Artistic director

Musician

Wardrobe assistant

Lighting technician

Dancer

*This is excluding classical ballet companies.

Artistic director

All companies have an artistic director. This is the person who invites choreographers, designers and musicians to work with the company and chooses the dances, or "programme", to be performed. He or she also selects dancers to join the company and supervises their training.

In a small company the artistic director may also perform, take rehearsals and design costumes and lighting.

Company manager

This is the person who runs the company behind the scenes. He or she controls the company money. This includes paying dancers, negotiating contracts with choreographers and musicians and raising funds to support the company.

The company manager also finds places to rehearse, gets bookings at theatres, organizes tour arrangements and deals with last-minute crises, such as dancers injuring themselves or costumes getting lost.

Press and publicity officer

The press and publicity officer contacts theatres and discusses how to advertise the show, and gets posters and leaflets printed. He or she arranges interviews with the press and contacts local schools and dance centres to offer reduced price tickets.

The publicity officer also organizes the printing of programmes, t-shirts and badges which are often sold before the performance to promote the show.

The dancers

Dance companies are usually more democratic than ballet companies. There are no stars or principal ballerinas, so more dancers get the opportunity to perform solo or leading roles. In small companies five or six dancers perform every piece and there are no understudies or second casts. This puts the performers under more pressure but also gives them more work.

Dancers may also hold classes called workshops in local schools or dance centres to introduce the dances the company is performing.

Working with the rehearsal director

Rehearsal director

The rehearsal director's job is to make sure the dances are performed well on stage. He or she watches rehearsals of new pieces, discussing the works with the choreographer and teaching new dancers their roles.

On tour the rehearsal director takes a rehearsal on stage in each different theatre, to work out how pieces will be performed on that particular stage. He or she also keeps the company up to scratch by taking notes at each performance and giving them to the dancers the next day so they can make corrections.

Checking the lights

Stage manager

This is the person responsible for getting the set built and the costumes made. He or she also makes sure the lighting and sound are ready for the performance, and that the scenery is properly in place. The stage manager also works out the rehearsal schedule.

On tour the stage manager discusses with each theatre manager the lighting and stage space needed for the dances.

Wardrobe manager

The wardrobe manager makes and maintains the dancers' costumes, washing and mending them. He or she needs to be able to sew skilfully and make costumes according to a designer's sketches.

In small companies dancers often make the costumes themselves.

Staging a dance

Staging a dance means getting it ready to perform to an audience. This involves much more than rehearsing the movements: normally, the dance needs lighting, costumes and a set. These add a lot to the performance.

Preparations

The lighting, set, and costume designers work closely with the choreographer while the dance is being prepared. However it is not until the dance is nearly due to be performed that all the different elements are brought together.

In the week before the first performance, there is a special technical rehearsal on the stage. The dancers "mark" out their movements so that the designers can check that the lighting, sound and set fit exactly with the dance.

Then there is a dress rehearsal where the dance is performed exactly as if to an audience, with the dancers wearing their costumes. This is an exciting moment: everyone sees the overall effect of the dance for the first time. It is also the last chance to change things that do not work.

The **proscenium arch** is the frame around the front of the stage.

Scenery

The **backdrop** is a large canvas cloth which hangs at the back of the stage. It is usually painted with a scene to create a background for the dance.

Tabs are curtains hung at the sides of the stage. They are sometimes drawn across the stage to separate it into different sections or to hide parts of it from the audience.

Wings are the spaces at the sides of the stage, in between the tabs. The dancers wait here to go on stage. When they stand in the wings they are hidden from the audience.

The stage

Dance stages vary from elaborate structures with proscenium arches (see picture) to bare spaces containing only the dance floor and stage lights. Some stages are raised above floor level. Others are on the floor, with the audience seating "raked". This means it rises in tiers above the stage level.

The best size for a dance stage is from 10m (33ft) deep by 10m across to 15m (49ft) deep by 15m across. It should have a smooth, even surface. The stage area can be altered by moving the tabs, or by positioning flats (see picture) in different places. Very big stages may have sections which can be made to revolve, or raised or lowered to create different levels.

The lights hang from a grid high above the stage.

Flats are large wooden frames with canvas stretched tightly over them and tacked down. Scenes are painted on the canvas to create different settings for the dance. Flats stand on metal struts and can be moved round the stage.

Strut

Costumes

Lighting

The lighting for a dance should make the shapes of the dancers' bodies stand out, to show each movement clearly.

Different coloured lights help to create the moods in the dance, and suggest the time of day and the season in which it is happening. Red and amber give a warm feeling, while blue makes a cool, wintery impression.

The whole mass of lighting equipment is called the rig. The grid is the network of metal bars from which the lights, called lanterns, are hung.

An enormous range of lighting effects can be created using different types of lanterns.

Flood light

Profile spots, for example, give out strong beams of light which can focus on particular areas. Fresnel spots give a gentler light which covers a wide area. Flood lights produce wide beams.

Fresnel spot

Profile spot

Costumes

The most important thing about a dance costume is that it should let the dancer move freely. Dance costumes are often made of stretchy fabrics which outline the body shape and allow the dancer to move in any direction.

Costumes also affect the look of the dance movements. Light, flowing fabrics produce airy, graceful effects. Heavy fabrics cut in sharp shapes create a strong, more severe impression.

Special effects can be produced by decorating the costumes, for example with feathers or sequins. Brilliantly coloured costumes can give a dance a vivid impact.

The set

The set of a dance is made up of a backdrop, flats and scenery, such as tables and chairs. Its purpose is to suggest the place in which the dance is happening. A set is specially designed for each dance.

The set designer makes detailed plans and often builds a scale model of the set which helps to show what it will look like and how

it should be constructed. The full-size set is then built by skilled craftsmen.

Because dance fills a stage very well on its own, dance sets often use little more than a backdrop, coloured lighting effects and a few flats. The set must always leave plenty of room for the dancers to move around freely.

Sport and dance

Sport and dance are similar in many ways. Both build up your physical strength and teach you self-discipline. They help you move in a precise way. In dance you move accurately to make your meaning clear. In sports like tennis and baseball, the more precisely you move to hit the ball, the better you are at the sport. If you already play sport this will help you when you learn dance, just as doing dance will improve your sports skills.

Useful dance skills in sport

Dance increases your suppleness, helping you stretch further and bend more easily. This is an advantage in a sport like tennis where you have to stretch out suddenly to reach the ball.

Learning to dance shows you how to fit your body into different spaces, for example, how to move neatly in a small space, and how to reach up into the air. These skills help you in games like basketball, where you need to jump high and dodge round your opponents.

Dancing in groups helps you in team sports, by making you more aware of other people and how to fit your movements to theirs.

Dance in ice-skating and gymnastics

Two sports where dance has had a big influence are ice-skating and gymnastics. In both these sports, the body is treated almost as an object.

In gym it has to be twisted, stretched or thrown through the air and caught up again, almost like a rubber ball.

In skating the body has to be manipulated to make interesting patterns.

This approach means that although good skaters and gymnasts may be able to move in a way that is technically impressive, they do not always put a lot of feeling into their movements. Dance can help them add warmth and flair to their routines.

Dance and the martial arts

Sports such as judo, karate and Tai' Chi are called martial arts. They began in the Far East long ago as a means of self-protection, using the body as a weapon.* Like dance, they aim to develop control of the body and the mind together.

For this reason Tai' Chi particularly is now often learnt by contemporary dancers. It is a very graceful and controlled technique, with unusual movements. Just as words from foreign languages can sometimes express our ideas or feelings more clearly than our native language, contemporary dancers find that Tai' Chi can add expression and variety to their dance style, or "movement vocabulary".

*The word martial comes from Mars, the Roman god of war.

Dance therapy

Dance therapy is a form of treatment in which dance is used to help people who have mental and physical handicaps. It is also used to help people who have had difficulties in learning, or in fitting in to society, and to relieve people who are emotionally disturbed.

How dance therapy works

The theory behind dance therapy is that the mind and body cannot be thought of as two completely separate things.

Your state of mind affects your body, and your physical health affects your state of mind. If you are unhappy, you won't feel like running around or leaping in the air. Your movements will probably become slow and very small. And if your body is ill or injured, you will probably feel quite depressed.

Dance therapy helps you to release tension, fear or frustration by moving your body.

It helps people with physical handicaps such as blindness or deafness to communicate with other people. Dance is a kind of language using the body. When we are very young, before we learn to talk, we use movements to speak to people. In the same way, when people dance together in harmony, they are talking to one another through their bodies.

How different people benefit

Through dance, blind people can become aware of the size and shape of their bodies and how they can move in the space around them, so they move with more confidence. By dancing with other people they can also get to know through touch what they are like.

People who are deaf have trouble learning to speak because they cannot hear the sounds to imitate. Dance helps them communicate through gestures.

Mentally handicapped people often have difficulty in concentrating for long. This may stop them from learning new things. Because dance is fun, doing dance movements encourages them to get into the habit of concentrating longer. By repeating particular movements they learn how to remember them.

Gradually they are able to learn more complicated sequences and this helps develop the memory.

Blind people can gain confidence by doing movements with others.

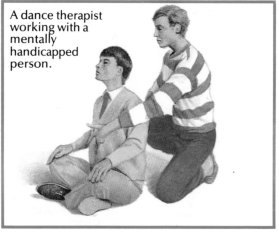

A dance therapist working with a mentally handicapped person.

Dance as a profession

To be a dancer you need a wide range of skills and a readiness to do all sorts of work, from performing in cabarets to appearing in TV commercials. There are very few opportunities to join dance companies and most dancers are freelance, taking whatever jobs come up and sometimes travelling abroad to find work.

Dance companies

Many dancers dream of joining a company. Large dance companies often have their own dance school. Each year they select just one or two of the dance students to join the company. The other dancers may find jobs in smaller companies, or form their own groups to get performing opportunities.

Musicals and shows

Some musicals, such as *A Chorus Line*, are performed by dancers. Dancers are often needed for seasonal shows too, such as Christmas pantomimes or summer shows at holiday resorts.

For musicals and shows you need to be trained in all kinds of dance and you often have to sing and act, too.

Cabaret

Cabaret acts usually involve a lot of dancing. They are performed in discos or night clubs. The acts are fast and energetic, lasting for only about 15 minutes each night. The dancers may also perform feats such as fire-eating.

Cruise ships employ dancers to perform in cabarets to entertain passengers.

Musicals

Shows

Film

Advertising

TV

Video

TV and film

You often see dancers backing singers or other entertainers in TV shows. Some TV dramas and films require dancers as extras. Since the 1970s there have been some very popular films about dancers, including *Saturday Night Fever*, *Flashdance*, *Footloose*, *Beat Street*, *A Chorus Line* and *Fast Forward*.

Pop videos

The pop videos made by bands to promote their records in discos and on TV provide another source of dance jobs. In these videos dancing is often combined with skilful camera work to create exciting images.

Because pop videos vary a lot, the dancers may get the chance to do several different styles of dance.

Business

Advertising companies use dancers in television commercials to promote products such as paint, drinks or sweets. Clothes designers also sometimes use dancers to launch their new collections at fashion shows.

These jobs can be very interesting, especially if you get work in a variety of adverts or shows.

Training

Most dancers start their training by taking ballet classes when they are young. Ballet technique is a good basis for any kind of dance. Some students even attend full-time ballet school before switching to dance.

If you want to join a dance company you must train for several years at a dance school, which you can join at about 16 or 17 years old. The competition for places is fierce.

For work in musicals and shows you need a wide range of performing skills, including acting and singing as well as dancing. You can get this kind of general theatre training at special theatre schools which take pupils from the age of about 11 or 12.

Finding work

A dancer with a company has regular work, but in other fields the work is intermittent. A job may last for one day, or a few weeks, or for months.

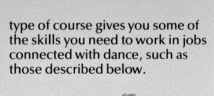

To get jobs, dancers attend auditions. These are rather like interviews where you perform in front of a panel of selectors who are looking for dancers to work in a particular show, video or TV commercial.

Many dancers pay an agent to get auditions for them. Dancers who do not have an agent have to find out about auditions for themselves, either from dance magazines and newspapers or by word of mouth.

Other careers in dance

Not everybody wants or is able to be a professional dancer. It is now possible to study dance as an academic subject as well as a performing art, learning about its history, its role in society, the art of choreography, dance notation, dance criticism and anatomy. This type of course gives you some of the skills you need to work in jobs connected with dance, such as those described below.

Administration

Dance administration is the work involved in running a dance company or dance centre or theatre. This includes organizing the finances and for this kind of work you may need a business qualification as well as a knowledge of dance.

Teaching

Dance is widely taught in schools, colleges and dance or sports centres. You can get specialist teaching qualifications, but these are not always necessary. A new job related to teaching is that of "dance animateur". This is someone who visits schools, community centres and old people's homes, introducing dance to all age groups and encouraging interest in it as a creative activity.

Dance therapy

Dance therapists work in hospitals and special schools. They use dance to help handicapped people (see page 91).

Dance therapy is a fairly new field but there are a few training courses available.

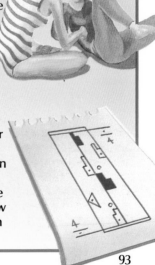

Dance notation

Dance notators write down dances as they are being created. Being a dance notator is a highly skilled job and you need to take a special course in notation. These courses are available at centres such as the Dance Notation Bureau in New York or the Benesh Institute in London.

Dance words

Afro-Caribbean dance. A kind of dance which developed over many centuries in the Caribbean islands, from a combination of traditional African and European folk dancing. Afro-Caribbean dance has influenced jazz dance.

Alignment. The way you hold your body when you are dancing to create a graceful line.

Amalgamation. A term used in dance to describe a sequence which combines different kinds of steps.

Animateur. A dance teacher who goes to schools and community centres to introduce dance to people of various age groups.

Balance. A dance term which describes both holding your body in a stable position, and also the inner feeling that your body is working as a controlled whole as you move.

Ballet. A stylized, formal type of performance dancing. Ballet aims to create graceful patterns and involves rigorous training.

Ballroom dance. A popular form of dance done in couples. It was widely danced from the 1930s to the 1950s and is still done socially and for competitions.

Benesh notation. A code of symbols used to write down dance movements. It was invented by Rudolf and Joan Benesh.

Body popping. A kind of breakdancing where you move different bits of your body separately.

Breaking. An energetic, quite dangerous form of breakdancing where you do moves such as headspins.

Broadway jazz. A jazz dance style which has influenced the dancing you see in TV and stage shows.

Centre of movement. The dance term for the mid-point of your body from which dance movements start.

Centrework. Usually the second stage of a class in *Graham technique*, involving exercises done standing up.

Choreographer. A person who creates dances.

Choreography. The art of creating dances.

Choreologist. A person who writes down dances using a form of *dance notation*.

Choreology. The art of writing down dance movements in *dance notation*.

Contraction. A dance movement which involves tightening the stomach muscles in order to help the pelvis and spine move more freely.

Cooling down. The process of doing gentle stretching exercises after dancing so that your muscles relax gradually. This helps to stop you becoming stiff the next day.

Co-ordination. The way you combine movements so your body moves as a balanced whole, even though different parts may be doing different things.

Cunningham technique. A style of contemporary dance developed by the American dancer, Merce Cunningham.

Dance notation. A code of written symbols used for recording dance steps on paper. The most commonly used systems of notation are *Labanotation* and *Benesh notation*.

Dance slippers. Soft slip-on shoes with rubber or leather soles and soft leather or canvas uppers, which allow the foot to flex and point freely.

Demi-plié. A dance movement which involves bending your knees while keeping your heels on the floor.

Elevation. The ability to jump high into the air in dance.

Extension. The action of stretching out part of your body as far as you can.

Flexed foot. A position of the foot in which the ankle is bent and toes pulled back towards the knee.

Floorwork. Usually the first part of a class in *Graham technique*. It is done sitting, lying or kneeling on the floor.

Foxtrot. A popular ballroom dance which developed during the 1930s in America and involved quick, running movements across the dance floor. Some features of the Foxtrot were incorporated into jazz dance.

Gospel jazz. A special kind of jazz dance which is done to traditional gospel music like that sung by the black slaves in America in the 17th and 18th centuries.

Graham technique. A style of contemporary dance developed by the American dancer, Martha Graham.

Improvisation. Dancing or acting without having set steps or a script and with little advance preparation. Improvisation is used to explore different ways of expressing ideas in movement.

Isolation. A movement used in several styles of dance, such as jazz and breakdancing. It involves moving one part of the body separately from the rest of it.

Jitterbug. One of the earliest forms of jiving which was popular in America in the 1930s and '40s.

Jiving. A type of energetic rock 'n' roll dancing.

Labanotation. A code of symbols invented by Rudolf von Laban for writing down dance moves.

Limón technique. A style of contemporary dance developed by the Mexican dancer, José Limón.

Lock. The action of straightening the knee fully when you are standing up, so that your leg provides a strong support for your weight.

Long. A term used in dance to mean keeping a part of the body such as your neck or back stretched out straight, but not stiff.

Marking. Going through the movements of a dance routine without dancing them fully, in order to familiarize yourself with the steps before performing. Dancers also mark steps in a technical rehearsal, to show the lighting and sound technicians which parts of the stage will be used in the dance.

Movement memory. A term used in dance therapy to describe the sequences of movements a person can remember how to do.

Movement vocabulary. The range of different movements a dancer can do.

Moving in space. The part of a contemporary dance class where you do movements that take you across the dance studio.

Opposition. Moving opposite sides of the body at the same time. In the *triplet* on page 61, for example, your left arm swings forward as you step on to your right leg. The term can also describe arm positions in which the arms point in opposite directions.

Parallel. A dance position in which you stand with your feet and legs facing in the same direction, either close together or apart.

Pattern. A term used in tap dancing to describe the overall shape of a dance sequence.

Plié. A dance movement in which you bend your knees fully until you are very near the ground, with your heels off the floor.

Post-modern dance. The various kinds of contemporary dance which have evolved since the 1960s.

Release. A dance term for straightening the spine out of a *contraction*. The release should not be a collapse of the muscles. In a release position your back is completely straight.

Relevé. A dance movement in which you rise up on to the balls of your feet.

Routine. In dance, a term meaning a sequence of movements or steps.

Stamina. Your ability to sustain physical activity over a long time.

Stop timing. A term used in tap dancing when a dancer stops moving and holds a position while the music goes on playing.

Synchronization. Doing different movements at the same time, for example, clapping your hands while moving your feet.

Syncopation. The marking out of beats in a rhythm so that you bring out unexpected parts of the rhythm, for example, clapping in between the strong beats of a rhythm.

Tacit timing. A term used in tap dancing to describe a moment when the music stops and the dancers go on dancing, so that only the sound of their tapping can be heard.

Tempo. The speed at which a dance is performed or music is played.

Tilt. A dance position where you hold your body at an angle to your supporting leg.

Time step. A set rhythm or pattern of steps tapped out by your feet in tap dancing. Time steps are usually repeated several times and so used in routines to lead into more spectacular movements.

Timing. The way the movements of a dance fit the accompanying rhythm or music.

Traditional jazz. A type of jazz dancing which developed in America from vaudeville and minstrel shows.

Transition steps. Movements done in between different positions in a dance sequence or exercise.

Travelling step. A step in which you move across the floor.

Triplet. A dance walk done to a 3/4 beat.

Turned out. Term used to describe a dance position in which you stand with your legs and feet facing outwards. Your feet may be either together or apart.

Uprock. A type of competitive breakdancing done by gangs in New York instead of fighting with weapons.

Warming up. Doing exercises which stretch and loosen the muscles to prepare your body for dancing.

Records for jazz dance

For rock jazz

Almost any records by the following:

Michael Jackson
Grace Jones
Donna Summer
"Wham"
"Five Star"
Madonna
Matt Bianco

Songs from the albums *Jump* by the Pointer Sisters and *Let's Dance* by David Bowie.

Songs from *Fame, Flashdance, West Side Story, A Chorus Line* and *Cats.*

For funk jazz

Most records by:

Quincy Jones
Earth, Wind and Fire
George Benson

For soul jazz

Any records by:

Womack and Womack
Aretha Franklin
Sade
Stevie Wonder
Smokey Robinson

For traditional jazz

Take Five by Dave Brubeck
Sing Sing Sing by Benny Goodman

Any records by Duke Ellington (although these are probably too difficult for beginners).

Index

Usborne Publishing would like to thank the following for use of photographs and other material for artistic reference. Every effort has been made to trace other photographers whose pictures have been used for reference.

Page 2, bottom left and centre © Anthony Crickmay; bottom right © Martha Swope. Page 12, top centre and page 13, Benesh Movement Notation © Rudolf Benesh London 1955. Page 18, bottom left © Roy Round; bottom right © Dominic Photography; illustration of a scene from the film "The Tales of Beatrix Potter" by kind permission of The Cannon Group UK Limited. Page 19, bottom left © Leslie E. Spatt. Page 20, top left © Camilla Jessel; top right © Martha Swope. Page 38, top, bottom right and left © Leslie E. Spatt; centre © Camilla Jessel. Page 43, top centre © Leslie E. Spatt; bottom centre © Dominic Photography. Page 44, centre © Leslie E. Spatt. Page 45, right © Roy Round. Page 50, centre left © Dominic Photography. Page 52, top © Pineapple Group plc. Page 56, top © Pineapple Group plc. Page 59, bottom centre © Anthony Crickmay. Page 84, top right © BBC Hulton Picture Library. Page 85, top © Dominic Photography; centre right © Anthony Crickmay.

First published in 1987 by Usborne Publishing Ltd, 83-85 Saffron Hill, London EC1N 8RT.